THE ABANDONED CRICKET BAT

Mehul V. Mane

MVM
Writings

First Edition Published [October 2025]

ISBN: 978-93-344-3987-8 (Paperback)

Acknowledgement

This book is the result of countless hours of solitary effort, reflection, and persistence. It was written in silence and brought to life through my own dedication and determination. Every page reflects not only the story within, but also the discipline and passion that guided me throughout the journey of creating it.

Though no one knew of its existence until now, this novel stands as a testament to what can be accomplished through perseverance and an unwavering belief in one's vision. I extend my deepest gratitude to the readers who will embark on this journey through these pages, your time and attention give this work its true purpose.

Contents

Chap. 01 ~ The Bat in the Dust 1

Chap. 02 ~ The Forgotten Prodigy 15

Chap. 03 ~ Echoes in the Pavilion 29

Chap. 04 ~ The Syndicate's Shadow 43

Chap. 05 ~ Beneath the Floodlights 57

Chap. 06 ~ The Charity Gambit 70

Chap. 07 ~ Threads of Deception 84

Chap. 08 ~ The Net Tightens 98

Chap. 09 ~ Breaking the Silence 113

Chap. 10 ~ The Siege Begins 127

Chap. 11 ~ Regroup and Retaliate 142

Chap. 12 ~ Consolidating the Evidence 157

Chap. 13 ~ The Final Confrontation 172

Chap. 14 ~ Aftermath and Reflection 187

Chap. 15 ~ New Beginnings 201

Chap. 16 ~ Confrontation and Resolution 217

CHAPTER : 1

THE BAT IN THE DUST

The monsoon had returned to Pune, painting the streets in hues of wet asphalt and fogged lights. The air was thick with the smell of damp earth, rotting leaves, and the occasional whiff of chai from roadside stalls. Beyond the noisy traffic and neon billboards, there lay an abandoned cricket pavilion in Deccan Gymkhana, forgotten by time. Its white paint was peeling, and the wooden beams creaked as though groaning under the weight of memories long gone. Few dared to enter the structure; stories of snakes, rusted metal, and the vanished boy prodigy circulated among locals, keeping curiosity at bay.

That evening, a group of boys, their clothes muddied from play, squeezed through the sagging gate, their laughter echoing through the hollow space. Among them was Aditya, the tallest of the group, who carried a worn tennis ball. He tripped on a patch of loose soil, sending a small cloud of dust into the air. When he tried to pull his foot free, his fingers brushed against something solid buried beneath the mud.

“Hey… what’s this?” he asked, crouching.

The others gathered, eyes wide. Together, they began digging with bare hands, pulling away the earth until a wooden object emerged. It was a cricket bat - old, scarred, its grip frayed, the willow darkened with age.

But it was the name carved just below the splice that made their hearts stop: Vihaan Palkar.

The boys froze. Vihaan Palkar, the cricket prodigy who had vanished twenty years ago, was more legend than man. The air seemed to still around them, as if the pavilion itself was holding its breath.

Aditya ran his fingers over the faded engraving, tracing each letter. “Do you think… he really played here?”

Rohit, younger and more daring, grinned nervously. “Maybe. Or maybe it’s cursed.”

By the next morning, the news of the bat had swept through Pune like wildfire. The abandoned pavilion, once a ghostly relic, was now a magnet for curiosity. Locals gathered in small clusters, whispering tales of Vihaan Palkar, the boy prodigy whose name had become legend. Phones clicked incessantly, capturing images of the mud-stained bat, while social media buzzed with posts, hashtags, and debates. One photo, slightly blurred but compelling, carried the caption: *“The Ghost of Pune’s Cricket Past.”*

In her tiny flat in Shivajinagar, Avni Mhatre scrolled through her phone with a mixture of disbelief and excitement. The sight of Vihaan’s name carved into the bat sent a shiver down her spine. She remembered watching him in stadiums as a child, his elegance with the bat, the roar of the crowd, the endless replayed footage on television. Memories of youthful arguments over his fate, whether he had vanished, been silenced, or run away came flooding back.

Avni's current life felt trivial in comparison. Her career as a journalist had stalled; freelancing for clickbait websites barely paid the rent, and her once-promising reputation was fading. But this discovery, it was different. Tangible. Real. Alive.

She grabbed her worn notebook, flipping past abandoned story ideas and unpaid pitches. Her eyes landed on an old draft titled *"The Unsolved Mystery of Vihaan Palkar."* Her pulse quickened. This could be the story that pulled her from obscurity, the one that could revive her career and uncover a truth that had been buried for two decades.

For the first time in months, Avni felt a spark of hope. She typed a message to a trusted colleague:

> *"Meet me near Deccan Gymkhana. Bring your camera. Something big has surfaced – Vihaan Palkar's bat."*

The city's rain-soaked streets seemed to hum with anticipation, and somewhere in the distance, the ghost of Pune's cricket past stirred.

By afternoon, the abandoned pavilion at Deccan Gymkhana had become a small spectacle. The drizzle had slowed to a fine mist, and Pune's monsoon-soaked streets reflected the soft glow of streetlights and neon shop signs. Locals, reporters, and curious onlookers jostled for position, craning to see the bat that had resurfaced after twenty years.

Avni navigated through the crowd, her press badge swinging from her neck. She had worn faded jeans and a black kurta, trying to blend in, but her eyes were fixed on the bat. It rested on a makeshift pedestal, carefully dusted and positioned under the weak shelter of the pavilion's roof. Its surface was scarred, edges worn, but the name Vihaan Palkar gleamed faintly, as if defying time itself.

More than the name, Avni noticed a series of faint initials and dates etched along the bat's length: *"A.T. – 1999," "S.J. – 2000," "V.S. – 2001."* They were not random scratches; they were deliberate, coded in a pattern that suggested someone had left them as clues. Her journalist instincts tingled. This wasn't just a relic, it was a breadcrumb trail.

She knelt, taking careful photographs, her fingers tracing the engraved letters. Her pulse quickened. Every scratch, every smudge, was potentially a lead, a message, or a warning. She scribbled notes furiously in her notebook, already mapping out possibilities.

A subtle unease prickled at her. Across the street, a tall figure leaned against a motorbike, pretending to be absorbed in his phone. Yet Avni felt the weight of his gaze. Someone was watching, perhaps more than one.

But there was no turning back now. The story had found her, and Avni knew that following these clues could change everything, for better or worse.

The crowd around the pavilion murmured in hushed tones. Older men spoke of Vihaan Palkar's genius at the crease, the precision of his shots, and the way he had carried the hopes of an entire city on his shoulders. Their voices trembled, not from fear, but from the memory of loss. Children, oblivious to the weight of history, poked the mud around the pedestal, fascinated by the bat's worn handle and the faint engravings.

Avni approached a small cluster of elderly spectators. She introduced herself, her voice steady but curious. "Do you remember him - Vihaan Palkar?" she asked.

One man adjusted his fogged spectacles and nodded slowly. "We all remember him. He was magic. Every time he came to the crease, you could feel the whole stadium hold its breath. And then… he was gone. Just like that."

Another chimed in, voice hushed, "Some say he refused to throw a match. Others say the world moved on too fast, and he disappeared under its weight. No one knows what really happened that night."

Avni's pen moved quickly, capturing every word, every hesitation, every nuance. She could feel the story forming, like invisible threads weaving a tapestry of brilliance, betrayal, and disappearance.

Yet, a subtle tension lingered. The initials on the bat, combined with these recollections, hinted at something more sinister. Someone had left messages, deliberately hidden in plain sight, perhaps hoping that a perceptive soul would follow.

Avni glanced over her shoulder. The figure across the street was still there, leaning against the motorbike, eyes fixed on her. A shiver ran down her spine. The story was no longer just history, it was alive, and it was watching her.

She inhaled sharply, steadying her nerves. Tomorrow, she decided, she would start digging deeper, tracing every lead, every name, every date.

The monsoon drizzle continued, blending the past with the present in a curtain of mist, as if Pune itself was whispering secrets.

Avni crouched closer to the bat, her fingers lightly tracing the worn engravings. The letters were uneven, some deeper than others, as if carved in haste but with intention. *A.T. – 1999. S.J. – 2000. V.S. – 2001.* Each mark seemed like a breadcrumb, a coded trail waiting for someone determined enough to follow it.

She quickly opened her notebook and began mapping the initials and dates, connecting them with lines and arrows, forming a tentative web. Her mind raced with possibilities. Were they teammates? Coaches? Or individuals tied to something darker, perhaps match-fixing or political interference?

A few onlookers stared at her, murmuring. Some whispered about Vihaan's last match, the one that had ended abruptly after his record-breaking century. Others speculated about the night he vanished, the whispers growing more sinister with each telling. Avni absorbed every word, every nuance, knowing that even a fragment of truth could guide her to the bigger story.

Her journalist instincts pricked. Something about this bat was different. It wasn't just a relic; it was a message left deliberately, a bridge between the past and a secret someone desperately wanted to remain buried.

Avni glanced over her shoulder again. Across the street, the tall figure leaned casually against his motorbike, but his gaze never left her. A warning, or a threat, was clear in the way he lingered.

She closed her notebook, feeling both excitement and a twinge of fear. The discovery had pulled her into something larger than she had anticipated.

The rain continued to patter softly, washing the streets in silvery light. Avni stood, her resolve hardening. Whoever had left these clues, she would follow them. And she would uncover the truth, no matter the cost.

Avni stepped back, taking a moment to absorb the scene. The bat lay on its makeshift pedestal, a fragile artifact steeped in history and mystery. For a fleeting second, she let herself imagine Vihaan Palkar holding it, running his fingers along the worn handle, preparing for the innings that would never come.

Her own life felt trivial in comparison. At twenty-eight, she was a journalist clinging to the edges of relevance. Freelance articles for clickbait websites barely covered rent, and her once-promising career had stalled under the weight of rejections. Yet, this discovery stirred something deep within her, a spark of purpose she had long forgotten.

She pulled her notebook from her bag, flipping past rejected story pitches and half-finished drafts. Her eyes landed on an old, dog-eared page: *"The Unsolved Mystery of Vihaan Palkar."* The thought of reviving the story made her pulse quicken. This could be the investigation that would redefine her career—and perhaps uncover a truth long buried beneath the city's history.

Avni glanced once more at the bat, noting every scratch, every engraving, every smudge. The initials along the edge were deliberate. Someone had left a trail and she was determined to follow it.

A chill ran down her spine as she noticed movement across the street. The tall figure, leather jacket and motorbike, had not left. The man's posture was casual, almost indifferent, yet there was an unmistakable intensity in his gaze.

For the first time in years, Avni felt the thrill of being part of something bigger than herself. The bat was more than a story, it was a key. Somewhere in Pune, clues waited to be uncovered. And she had just crossed the threshold into a world where history, obsession, and danger intersected.

The drizzle had eased into a gentle mist, leaving Pune's streets glistening like polished silver. Avni closed her notebook and surveyed the pavilion one last time. The bat rested quietly on its pedestal, a silent witness to decades of rumors, theories, and unanswered questions. She knew that to unravel the mystery, she needed more than her observations and notes. She needed someone who had seen Vihaan Palkar up close, someone who had been there the night everything changed.

There was only one person: Coach Ashok Tilekar. The man was a legend in Pune's cricketing circles, Vihaan's mentor and confidant, yet he had retreated from public life after the prodigy's disappearance. Finding him would be difficult; convincing him to talk would be even harder.

Avni pulled out her phone and scrolled through her old contacts until she found a number she hadn't dialed in years. Her thumb hovered over the call button. Memories of her college days resurfaced, days when she had interviewed the coach, days when she had hung on every word about Vihaan's rise.

Finally, she pressed call.

The line rang, the sound echoing in her ear. After several tense moments, a gruff voice answered, cautious and measured. “Ashok Tilekar,” the voice said.

“Sir, this is Avni Mhatre,” she began, trying to keep her voice steady. “I need to speak with you about Vihaan Palkar. The bat… it’s been found.”

There was silence on the other end. Then came a low, weary sigh. “Some stories are buried for a reason,” he said slowly. “Be careful, Avni. Some truths… can get you killed.”

Her heart skipped a beat. The warning only fueled her determination. She knew she was stepping into dangerous territory, but the chance to uncover the truth, Vihaan’s story, the bat, the messages was worth the risk.

As she ended the call, Avni felt the weight of the night settle over the city. The hunt had officially begun.

Night had fallen over Pune, the city wrapped in the soft hum of monsoon rain. Avni returned to her flat, the streets glistening under the reflection of streetlights. The city felt alive yet secretive, as if it were holding its breath along with her. She laid her notebook on the table and spread out her scribbled notes, the initials, dates, and the details she had captured at the pavilion.

Each line, each mark on the bat seemed to pulse with meaning. Avni traced the paths she had drawn, imagining how they might connect to Vihaan’s teammates, coaches, and perhaps even individuals no one dared to name aloud. The thrill of a discovery mingled with a creeping sense of danger. Something about this story whispered that someone, maybe more than one person was watching her every move.

The memory of the tall figure across the street, the one leaning against the motorbike, returned to her mind. His presence had been subtle yet deliberate, almost theatrical. Avni had sensed it immediately, a silent warning embedded in the shadows. The realization that the hunt for truth might come with peril did little to dampen her resolve; if anything, it sharpened it.

She brewed a cup of tea, its steam curling upward as if carrying fragments of her thoughts. Her eyes moved across her notes, over the initials *A.T., S.J., V.S.*, over the dates that spanned two decades. Whoever had left these clues had done so with purpose, and she was determined not to let them go unanswered.

Avni stared out the window at the wet streets below, listening to the distant rumble of thunder. Tomorrow, she would take her first concrete steps, contact old sources, chase leads, and perhaps finally unlock the mystery of Vihaan Palkar. The game had begun, and she was already deep in play.

The night deepened, and the rain softened to a gentle drizzle, tapping against the windowpane in a rhythmic pattern. Avni sat hunched over her notebook, her pen racing across the pages. Every engraving on the bat seemed to carry a story, a fragment of a puzzle she was only beginning to understand. *A.T., S.J., V.S.,* the initials felt like markers left deliberately, guiding her toward a truth that someone had wanted to preserve, despite the years.

A sense of unease lingered. She couldn't shake the image of the man across the street, watching her at the pavilion. The memory of his casual posture, the way he had seemed to merge with the shadows, made her skin prickle. He hadn't moved, not once, until she left. Someone was clearly interested in her investigation, perhaps monitoring her from afar.

Her mind drifted to Vihaan. The boy who had carried the hopes of a city, who had been silenced before his moment of glory. The bat was more than an artifact; it was a message, a last piece of communication from a vanished life. And now it was in her hands, beckoning her to uncover the hidden truths behind its scars.

Avni sipped her tea, her thoughts spinning with possibilities. She knew that following this story might place her in danger. The warning from Ashok Tilekar lingered in her ears: *"Some truths... can get you killed."* But the desire to uncover the mystery outweighed fear.

Somewhere in the city, shadows shifted, watching. Somewhere, someone waited. And somewhere, a story that had been buried for decades was waiting to be unearthed.

Avni's fingers tightened around her pen. Tomorrow, she would chase it, no matter the cost. The first moves of a dangerous game were already underway.

Avni spread her notes across the small table, the scattered pages filled with initials, dates, and hastily drawn lines connecting names and events. The bat's markings had ignited a fire in her mind, each scratch and groove suggesting secrets someone had tried to leave behind, hoping a perceptive soul would follow. She studied the patterns, imagining the possible connections between Vihaan, his teammates, and unknown players in the shadows of Pune's cricketing world.

The memory of Ashok Tilekar's voice echoed in her head: *"Some truths... can get you killed."* The warning was not abstract anymore, it felt immediate, like the faint pressure of eyes on her back. The thought of danger should have frightened her, but instead, it sharpened her resolve. She was ready to chase the story wherever it led, no matter how treacherous the path.

Avni's gaze drifted to the rain-soaked streets outside her window. The city seemed different at night, alive with secrets and hidden movements. Somewhere in Pune, the next clue awaited, buried beneath layers of time and silence. The bat had opened a door, and she could no longer turn away.

She picked up her pen, poised to chart the next steps. Tomorrow, she would visit old contacts, search archives, and begin tracing the people connected to those initials. Every instinct screamed that she was on the edge of something monumental.

A distant rumble of thunder punctuated her thoughts. The storm mirrored the turmoil building inside her, excitement, fear, anticipation. The game had begun, and Avni was already a player. She leaned back, took a deep breath, and whispered to herself:

I will find the truth. No matter what it takes.

The monsoon's patter against the window seemed almost like applause, a city's subtle acknowledgment that a story long buried had finally found its seeker.

CHAPTER : 2

THE FORGOTTEN PRODIGY

Pune had changed over the past two decades, but some memories refused to fade. For Avni, Vihaan Palkar's name conjured images of sun-drenched stadiums, the crack of willow on leather, and the cheers of crowds that had once celebrated him like a deity. She closed her eyes and could almost hear the commentary from that final televised match, the one that had ended in chaos, and the night Vihaan disappeared without a trace.

Determined to understand the boy behind the legend, Avni began her research the next morning. She started at the city library, leafing through yellowed newspapers and old sports magazines. Articles celebrated Vihaan's meteoric rise: a prodigy who had shattered school records, captivated audiences in local leagues, and earned a place in the national squad before turning twenty. Each headline painted him as fearless, unyielding, a young man whose ambition had been matched only by his talent.

But there were cracks between the lines, subtle hints that all was not as perfect as it seemed. Rumors of pressure from coaches, whispers of conflicts with teammates, and speculation about shady figures lurking around key matches. Avni's pen moved swiftly, capturing details that seemed inconsequential at first, but in her gut, she felt they were pieces of a much larger puzzle.

Her next stop was Deccan Gymkhana itself, now quieter than yesterday. The pavilion, though abandoned, still exuded an air of reverence. She photographed the structure, noting its crumbling walls, the overgrown pitch, and the faded lines of the field. Somewhere within these decaying remnants, the essence of Vihaan's story lingered, waiting for someone to piece it together.

Avni's mind raced. If the bat had resurfaced after twenty years, then the trail wasn't cold, it was being actively maintained. Someone wanted her to find it.

Avni settled into a quiet corner of the library, flipping through archives from Vihaan's final season. The more she read, the more the prodigy's brilliance shone and the more mysterious the circumstances of his disappearance became. Match reports praised his skill, noting centuries scored under impossible pressure. Fans adored him, coaches trusted him implicitly, and yet, behind the headlines, something was off.

Her eyes paused on one match report: Vihaan had scored a record-breaking century, only for the game to be abruptly called off due to "unforeseen circumstances." No further explanation had been given. The silence around that night was deafening. Avni jotted down the date, her mind buzzing with questions. Who had stopped the match? Why had no one talked about it?

Next, she contacted a few former teammates still living in Pune. Some were hesitant, their voices shaking when Vihaan's name came up. One former teammate, Rohit Deshmukh, finally spoke after repeated calls. "Vihaan… he was a genius, yes, but there were pressures. People around him… they weren't all cricket lovers. Some were… interested in other things. Money. Control."

Avni's pulse quickened. Match-fixing? Betting syndicates? Could it really be connected to the initials carved on the bat?

Her notebook was filling fast, a web of names, dates, and possibilities. But a pattern was beginning to emerge: Vihaan had been more than a player; he had been a threat to someone's power.

Looking out the library window, Avni noticed the city's familiar chaos, buses honking, street vendors calling out, kids splashing in puddles. Beneath it all, the past whispered through the present. Somewhere, the truth waited. And for the first time, Avni felt that she was closing in on it.

After hours in the library, Avni left, notebook tucked under her arm, and walked toward the streets of Pune she had known since childhood. The city was alive with monsoon energy, vendors shouting over the splashes of tires in waterlogged roads, children kicking up puddles, and the faint scent of street-side chai mingling with wet earth. Yet, in the midst of life's chaos, a shadow of Vihaan's past lingered.

Her first stop was an old tea stall near the Nehru Stadium, where retired players and enthusiasts often gathered. Avni hoped to speak with those who had been closest to Vihaan. She found a few men huddled over steaming cups, their cricket anecdotes lively yet tinged with sadness.

“Vihaan?” she asked gently, showing a picture from her notebook. The men exchanged glances, their smiles tight.

“He was… different,” said one, voice low. “Not just skill, but instinct. He could read the game before anyone else.”

Another added, hesitantly, “Some nights, before matches, he would disappear from the hotel. No one knew where he went. And there were people… men who would show up, asking questions, watching him too closely. Something wasn’t right.”

Avni scribbled furiously, connecting the dots with her notes on the bat. Every mention of mysterious men, sudden disappearances, and unusual pressures made a troubling pattern emerge. It was no longer just a missing player, it was a story of secrets, fear, and possibly danger.

She looked around the tea stall, noting the faces and expressions. Some men avoided eye contact, hands fidgeting nervously. Others whispered to each other. Whoever had watched Vihaan then might still be watching now.

The bat, the initials, the vanished prodigy, it all pointed to something far larger than a simple story. Avni knew she had to tread carefully. The investigation had begun, and the first real threads of a dark conspiracy were slowly unraveling before her.

From the tea stall, Avni made her way to a quieter part of Pune, to an old residential area where former players and coaches still lived. The streets were narrow, lined with tall banyan trees dripping from the recent rain. Each step seemed to echo with the city's cricketing past, and she felt a strange connection to the memories Vihaan had left behind.

Her destination was a small, faded house belonging to a former teammate, Sanjay Joshi. Avni had contacted him earlier, and after some persuasion, he had agreed to meet. She found him sitting on a veranda, fanning himself despite the drizzle, a cricket bat propped against the wall beside him. His eyes widened slightly when she mentioned Vihaan's name, and for a moment, he seemed caught between nostalgia and unease.

"He… he was exceptional," Sanjay said quietly, taking a sip of tea. "But brilliance attracts attention. Not all of it good. The night before his debut… he received visitors. Important people, some from the board, some… I don't even know. They were persuasive, insistent. Vihaan refused something. That's when everything changed."

Avni leaned forward, heart racing. "What did he refuse?"

Sanjay shook his head. "I don't know exactly. But after that night, he was never the same. And the next day… he vanished. No calls, no letters, nothing. Just gone."

Avni scribbled furiously in her notebook. The pieces were aligning: mysterious visitors, pressure from the board, the bat with its cryptic markings. Someone had gone to great lengths to ensure Vihaan's story remained hidden.

Outside, the monsoon rain fell harder, drumming against the tin roofs. For Avni, the weight of the mystery deepened. She sensed she was approaching a truth far more dangerous than she had imagined.

Avni left Sanjay Joshi's house with a notebook brimming with details, her mind racing. The story of Vihaan Palkar was no longer just about a vanished prodigy, it was about unseen forces, hidden pressures, and perhaps corruption that had tainted the sport he loved.

As she walked through Pune's rain-soaked streets, she replayed every word from the tea stall and Sanjay's veranda. Visitors who arrived the night before Vihaan's debut, influential people whose names weren't recorded in public archives, someone had silenced him. And the bat, with its cryptic initials, was clearly meant to guide someone who was paying attention. Someone like her.

Her next step was to consult old match records and reports from newspapers covering that season. She settled into a quiet corner of the city archive, where rows of yellowed pages chronicled Pune's cricketing past. Names, scores, schedules, but buried within were anomalies: match cancellations, unexplained substitutions, and curious references to key players missing from games.

Every anomaly seemed insignificant on its own, but together they formed a pattern that suggested a system of manipulation. Avni's pen moved faster, connecting names and dates to the initials on the bat. *A.T., S.J., V.S.,* they weren't just random. They could indicate individuals involved in controlling outcomes, in protecting secrets that Vihaan had stumbled upon.

The city outside was quiet now, save for the occasional honk of a distant car and the steady patter of rain. Yet inside Avni, tension and excitement intertwined. This story was growing larger by the hour.

Someone had gone to extraordinary lengths to erase Vihaan Palkar, but the bat had reappeared, and with it, a trail that could expose the truth. Avni realized that following it might put her in danger, but she could not turn back now.

As Avni left the archives, Pune's streets had grown darker, slick with rain. Streetlights reflected on puddles like scattered stars, and the city seemed to hum with secrets. She sensed a presence again, the faint, almost imperceptible feeling that someone was following her. Each glance over her shoulder revealed only the usual nighttime passersby, yet instinct told her otherwise.

Back at her flat, she spread her notes and newspaper clippings across the table. The bat, the initials, the mysterious visitors, everything pointed toward a conspiracy more intricate than she had imagined. The pattern of cancellations, substitutions, and unexplained absences hinted at interference at multiple levels. The more she connected the dots, the clearer it became: Vihaan Palkar had been silenced for refusing to be part of something corrupt.

Her phone buzzed with a message from an unknown number:

"Stop digging. Some truths are dangerous."

Avni's pulse quickened. The warning confirmed her suspicions, someone was aware she was investigating, someone who wanted the past to remain buried. Her fingers trembled slightly as she held the phone, but fear was outweighed by determination.

She picked up the photograph of the bat and studied it again. Each initial, each date, each mark was now a piece of a puzzle that someone had intentionally left behind. Vihaan had wanted to communicate, to leave clues for a seeker brave enough to follow.

Avni leaned back, listening to the patter of rain on the window. The storm outside mirrored the tension in her mind. Danger lurked, but so did truth. And she was determined to uncover it, no matter how high the stakes, no matter who was watching.

Tomorrow, she would visit more former players and officials. The hunt had grown more urgent, and the city itself seemed to whisper warnings with every drop of rain.

The next morning, the monsoon had eased into a soft drizzle, leaving Pune's streets slick and reflective. Avni grabbed her bag, notebook, and camera, determined to follow the leads that were slowly taking shape. She had a plan: track down former associates of Vihaan Palkar, interview them carefully, and look for patterns connecting the initials on the bat to names in her notes.

Her first stop was an old cricket academy on the outskirts of the city, where Vihaan had trained in his early teens. The building was weathered, the paint peeling, but it still resonated with echoes of a bygone era. Inside, she found a retired groundskeeper, an elderly man named Dinesh, who remembered the prodigy vividly.

"He was unstoppable," Dinesh said, adjusting his spectacles. "But there were visitors… men in suits, unfamiliar faces at matches and practice sessions. They asked questions, observed him. Sometimes late at night, too. I never knew what they wanted, but Vihaan… he didn't like them. He resisted."

Avni scribbled every word, her mind connecting these accounts to the initials on the bat. *A.T., S.J., V.S.,* each letter seemed to correspond to figures who might have had influence over Vihaan's career, or worse, over the matches themselves.

Dinesh paused, lowering his voice. "Some people play for money, power, control. Vihaan… he wouldn't bend. That's why he disappeared. That's why… the bat exists."

A shiver ran down Avni's spine. The retired groundskeeper had unintentionally confirmed what she suspected: a syndicate had been manipulating events, and Vihaan's refusal had made him a target.

As she stepped back into the rain, Avni knew one thing for certain: uncovering the truth would be dangerous. But she also knew she had no choice. The chase had begun, and Pune's cricketing shadows were waiting.

Avni moved through Pune's rain-slicked streets, her notebook and camera secure in her bag. Every step reminded her that she was no longer simply following a story, she was stepping into a web of secrets that had ensnared Vihaan Palkar decades ago. The drizzling monsoon seemed to amplify every sound, from distant car horns to the splash of water under her shoes, and she felt eyes on her, though no one was immediately visible.

Her next destination was an old sports bar near Shivajinagar, known as a gathering place for former players and officials. Inside, the air smelled of strong chai and damp uniforms, and the hum of conversation paused as she approached. Avni displayed her press ID discreetly and asked if anyone remembered Vihaan Palkar's final matches.

A man in his sixties, former umpire Suresh Jadhav, beckoned her over. "You're asking about Vihaan?" he said cautiously. "Be careful. Not everyone wants the past disturbed."

She nodded, understanding the implicit warning. "I just need the truth, sir. Whatever you can tell me."

Suresh glanced around the room, lowered his voice, and spoke slowly. "There were names, initials… people with power in the board and betting networks. They controlled outcomes. Vihaan… he refused. That's when things went wrong. If you're digging, be careful. People notice. They always do."

Avni's stomach tightened. The threat was subtle but unmistakable. Yet her determination burned brighter. She took detailed notes, noting every name, every clue, and every subtle warning.

As she left the bar, the drizzle had thickened again, and a shadow flickered across her path. She felt the unmistakable sense that someone was following her, a silent reminder that uncovering the truth would not be easy, and that danger had already begun to shadow her steps.

Back at her flat, Avni spread out her notes, connecting the dots between the bat's initials and the people mentioned by Dinesh and Suresh. *A.T., S.J., V.S.,* each initial now seemed like a key to a hidden hierarchy, a network of individuals who had manipulated matches and silenced dissent. The pattern was becoming clearer, yet the deeper she went, the more dangerous the path appeared.

Her phone buzzed again, this time a call from an unknown number. She answered cautiously. A distorted voice whispered, *"Stop. Leave it alone. Or you'll regret it."*

The line went dead. Avni's hands trembled slightly, but she refused to be intimidated. Whoever had called knew she was following the trail. The syndicate, long hidden, was still active and watching.

She turned her attention back to the bat, the only tangible link to Vihaan's vanished life. The initials weren't just names, they were markers, breadcrumbs left for someone perceptive enough to find them. The realization hit her: Vihaan had intended this, anticipating that someone brave and intelligent would one day seek the truth.

Determined, Avni began mapping the initials against the former board members, players, and known figures involved in cricket betting networks. Each connection revealed new layers, implicating not just obscure operatives but powerful individuals whose influence stretched across Pune's cricketing world.

The rain outside intensified, drumming against her window as if urging her forward. Danger had arrived in the form of veiled threats and shadowed watchers, but Avni's resolve only strengthened. She would not turn back.

Tomorrow, she would confront more witnesses, track the initials further, and start piecing together the conspiracy that had destroyed Vihaan Palkar's career, and perhaps his life.

The city was alive, pulsating with secrets, and Avni knew she had already become part of its hidden currents.

The following morning, Avni's determination carried her to a small, nondescript office on the edge of Pune's business district. She had tracked down a former statistician, Ramesh Kulkarni, who had worked closely with the cricket board during Vihaan's final season. If anyone had access to detailed records, it would be him.

Ramesh greeted her cautiously, his gray hair disheveled and eyes darting nervously. "Vihaan Palkar," he muttered, almost in disbelief, as if the name itself carried danger. "I've tried to forget, but some things… they don't stay buried."

Avni leaned forward. "I need the truth, Mr. Kulkarni. The bat has resurfaced, and it has initials engraved A.T., S.J., V.S. Do these mean anything to you?"

Ramesh's hands trembled slightly as he adjusted his spectacles. "Those… those were people involved in controlling match outcomes, manipulating stats, influencing selections. Powerful, dangerous. They called themselves a syndicate, though no official records exist. Vihaan refused to cooperate… that's why he vanished."

Avni scribbled notes furiously, connecting the dots with her previous research. Every lead, every name, every oddity in the records now formed a sinister picture. The bat, the initials, the vanished prodigy, it was all part of a carefully hidden truth.

Her heart raced. She realized that uncovering this network could shake the very foundation of Pune's cricket world. Yet, danger was no longer abstract; it was tangible, lurking in every shadow, every unknown phone call, every figure she glimpsed watching her from a distance.

Ramesh's words lingered in her mind as she left the office. The syndicate was real. Vihaan had been silenced. And now, by following the trail of a bat left in the mud, Avni was walking straight into the heart of a decades-old conspiracy.

The city around her seemed heavier somehow, as if aware of the storm she had unleashed.

CHAPTER : 3

ECHOES IN THE PAVILION

That evening, Avni returned to the crumbling old pavilion where the bat had first been unearthed. The structure loomed against the dusk, its broken windows glowing faintly as streetlights flickered on. It was here, she realized, that everything had started and perhaps, where the past still whispered its truths.

She stepped inside cautiously, her flashlight beam slicing through the darkness. The pavilion smelled of mildew and rust, its walls covered in faded posters of long-forgotten matches. Somewhere in the silence, she could almost hear the echoes of a cheering crowd, the applause that had once carried Vihaan's name through the air.

The wooden benches creaked as she walked across them, and for a brief moment, Avni imagined the young prodigy sitting here, lacing his gloves, unaware that his career and his life were about to collapse. She knelt where the bat had been buried, brushing the dirt once more with her fingertips.

Suddenly, her light caught something wedged beneath the loose floorboards. Heart pounding, she pried them open. Inside lay a faded notebook, its leather cover cracked with age. She flipped through it carefully: rough sketches of cricket fields, numbers, initials, some matching those on the bat. But there were also strange symbols, coded phrases, and a recurring line written in hurried strokes: *"They cannot silence everyone."*

Before she could read further, a sharp sound echoed through the pavilion, a footstep. Avni froze, her grip tightening on the notebook. She wasn't alone.

The darkness pressed in closer, and with it came the realization: her investigation had been noticed. Someone was following her, and the pavilion had become less a place of discovery and more a trap.

Avni steadied her breath, straining to separate the sounds of her own heartbeat from the faint rustle behind her. The pavilion was silent again, but silence itself was suspicious, like a predator crouched in wait. She turned slowly, her flashlight beam sweeping across the cracked walls and broken chairs.

"Who's there?" she called, her voice firm despite the tremor in her chest.

No reply. Only the faint echo of her own words bouncing back.

She slipped the notebook into her bag, zipping it tightly, and edged toward the exit. Her instincts screamed that the longer she stayed, the greater the danger. Then, a metallic glint caught her eye, a shadowy figure lingering by the far doorway, half-hidden in the gloom. The man didn't move, didn't speak, just stood there as though blocking her path.

Avni's pulse quickened. She weighed her options, confront him, flee, or bluff. Gathering her courage, she tightened her grip on the flashlight and strode toward the exit as if unbothered. When she came within a few steps, the figure shifted slightly, revealing a pair of watchful eyes under a hood.

"You're looking for ghosts best left buried," the man said in a low voice. His tone was calm, but there was an unmistakable menace beneath it.

Avni met his gaze without faltering. "Ghosts don't scare me. Lies do."

For a moment, the man seemed to study her, then stepped aside, allowing her to pass. But as she hurried into the night, Avni knew this was no act of kindness, it was a warning.

Someone wanted her to know she was being watched. And that, if she continued, the shadows of Pune's cricketing past would consume her next.

Back in her apartment, Avni locked the door behind her and double-checked the windows. The encounter in the pavilion still gnawed at her, why had the hooded man let her go? Was it a test, or a sign that her every move was already anticipated?

She pulled the faded notebook from her bag and placed it on the desk under a warm desk lamp. Its pages smelled of damp paper and time. She turned them one by one, carefully. Most were filled with cryptic notes: scores, coded initials, and diagrams of field placements. At first glance, they resembled the random jottings of a player. But the more she studied, the clearer it became, this was not about the game itself, but about manipulation.

Certain overs circled. Names reduced to initials, some familiar from the bat's engravings. And alongside them, sums of money scrawled hastily, like a ledger hidden within the pretense of cricket analysis.

One page, near the middle, stood out. In hurried handwriting, Vihaan had written: *"Pune, March 14, last chance. They want me to lose. Refused again. Coach says be careful. If I disappear, look beneath the pitch."*

Avni's breath caught. This wasn't just suspicion, it was Vihaan's voice, a cry for help recorded in ink. The note was dated the very night he vanished.

Her mind raced. *Look beneath the pitch.* The clue wasn't metaphorical, it was literal. The stadium, still active today, might be hiding what Vihaan had left behind.

As the realization struck, Avni's phone buzzed again. Another unknown number. She hesitated before answering.

This time, there was no distorted voice, only silence, heavy and deliberate, as though someone on the other end was listening to her breathe.

Avni ended the call abruptly, her nerves tingling. Whoever was on the other end hadn't spoken, but the silence itself was more threatening than words. Someone wanted her to know she was under watch, and worse, that they were close.

Still, she couldn't ignore Vihaan's words in the notebook: *"Look beneath the pitch."* That clue burned in her mind like a beacon. If there was anything hidden at the stadium, it could be the key to unraveling everything, the syndicate, Vihaan's disappearance, and the chain of threats that now circled her.

By midnight, Avni had made up her mind. She dressed in dark clothes, pulled on a hooded jacket, and packed only the essentials: a small flashlight, gloves, her recorder, and the notebook. Her journalist instincts warned her this was reckless, but the stronger voice within, the one that craved truth, pushed her forward.

The Pune International Stadium loomed like a silent giant under the dim glow of scattered floodlights. Security was light, only a few guards at the gates, and she had already mapped a side entrance from previous assignments. She slipped in through a service alley, her footsteps muffled by the damp ground.

The stadium felt hauntingly different at night, no roaring crowds, only the echo of her movements against the vast concrete bowl. She made her way down toward the pitch, the very heart of the ground, and knelt at its edge.

Her gloved hands brushed the soil. It looked freshly turned in places, uneven, as though something had been disturbed. She reached for her small trowel, her pulse quickening with every scrape of dirt.

Whatever Vihaan had hidden here was waiting for her.

Avni's hands worked steadily, though her heart hammered against her ribs. Each scrape of the trowel against the packed soil felt louder than it should, echoing in the stillness of the empty stadium. She paused often, glancing over her shoulder, but the only sounds were the faint hum of the floodlights and the distant barking of a stray dog outside the gates.

After several minutes, her tool struck something solid. Avni froze, her breath catching. She brushed the soil aside, and the outline of a small metal box emerged. Its edges were rusted, but it had clearly been buried with care, not discarded.

With trembling hands, she pried it loose and set it on the grass. The lock was corroded, brittle with age, and after a few forceful strikes with the trowel, it snapped open. She lifted the lid slowly.

Inside lay a stack of folded papers wrapped in a cloth. The smell of damp and ink wafted upward. She carefully unwrapped them, old letters, lists of names, match schedules annotated with strange symbols, and at the bottom, a faded photograph.

Her breath caught again. The photo showed Vihaan Palkar, smiling, arm slung around Coach Ashok Tilekar. Both looked younger, vibrant with purpose. But scribbled across the back in shaky handwriting were words that chilled her: *"Trust no one from the board. They will erase me."*

Avni's fingers trembled as she tucked the papers and photo into her bag. This was no longer just a story, it was evidence.

But as she rose to her feet, a sharp sound cracked through the silence: the metallic click of a flashlight being switched on behind her.

She wasn't alone.

The beam of the flashlight cut through the darkness, blinding Avni for a moment. She instinctively shielded her eyes, clutching the bag close to her chest. A voice followed, calm, deliberate, with a tone that carried authority.

"You shouldn't be here, Ms. Mhatre."

Her stomach knotted. The man stepped forward, the light lowering enough for her to glimpse his face. Inspector Jamkar.

Relief flickered for a second, but it was quickly replaced by suspicion. Was he here as an ally or a sentinel for the very people she was investigating?

“You’ve been watching me,” Avni said, her voice steady despite her racing pulse.

Jamkar’s eyes narrowed slightly. “And with good reason. You’re meddling in something bigger than you realize. Digging where you shouldn’t dig. Do you even understand what you’ve uncovered tonight?”

Avni tightened her grip on the bag. “Evidence. Proof that Vihaan Palkar was silenced. Isn’t that what you’re supposed to want, justice?”

A faint smile tugged at the inspector’s lips, though it held no warmth. “Justice is a slippery word. What you’ve got there could ruin men who sit higher than you imagine. Politicians, board members, players you still cheer for. They won’t hesitate to erase anyone who threatens them.”

His words carried both warning and veiled threat. Avni couldn’t tell whether he meant to protect her or scare her off.

“Then why are you here?” she asked cautiously.

Jamkar stepped closer, lowering his voice. “Because I don’t know yet if you’re reckless… or useful. That box might be the key, but holding it could also sign your death warrant.”

The silence stretched, heavy with unspoken intent.

Avni's pulse quickened, but she forced herself to meet Inspector Jamkar's gaze. His eyes were sharp, unreadable, as if weighing every word she might speak. The faint hum of the floodlights overhead only heightened the tension, making the stadium feel like an interrogation chamber.

"You talk like you know more than you're admitting," Avni said, her voice quiet but firm.

Jamkar smirked faintly. "Knowing and surviving are not the same thing. People who ask too many questions about Vihaan Palkar tend not to last long. Ask Coach Tilekar. Oh wait, you can't. Not anymore."

The reference struck Avni like a blow. She remembered the coach's sudden death, officially listed as a heart attack. But now, hearing Jamkar's words, it felt less like coincidence and more like a warning wrapped in fact.

"Are you saying he was killed?" Avni pressed, her grip tightening on the bag.

Jamkar's smirk faded. "I'm saying he got too close. Just like you." He paused, stepping nearer, lowering his voice to a near whisper. "But unlike him, you still have a choice. Walk away, burn your notes, forget this ghost story. Or keep digging and find out how deep this rot goes. And if you choose the second… you'll need someone who knows where the bodies are buried."

Avni's eyes narrowed. "Are you offering to help me, or warning me?"

The inspector studied her for a long moment before replying. "Both."

He turned abruptly, the beam of his flashlight swinging away, leaving her in half-shadow. "Decide quickly, Ms. Mhatre. They already know you've found the box."

The words chilled her more than the night air.

Avni hurried out of the stadium, her bag pressed tightly against her side. The weight of the metal box and its contents felt heavier than stone, as though she were carrying a live fuse ready to ignite. Jamkar's words lingered in her mind: *"They already know you've found the box."* That meant her time was limited.

She reached her flat just past two in the morning. Exhausted but restless, she locked every bolt and drew the curtains before setting the box on her desk. Her reflection in the window looked pale, her eyes wide with both fear and defiance.

The papers inside were fragile, but she unfolded them carefully. The lists of names included not only board members but also initials of players still active today, athletes idolized by millions. Some entries were marked with monetary figures that dwarfed anything she'd ever imagined. It was a ledger of betrayal, hidden in plain sight within cricket's sacred world.

The photograph of Vihaan and Coach Tilekar haunted her most. On the back, beneath the warning, was another faint scrawl she had missed earlier: *"If not me, then you."*

The words felt directed at her, though written decades ago. Was Vihaan anticipating that someone would eventually carry his burden?

Avni rubbed her temples, overwhelmed by the implications. If she published this too soon, she could be silenced before the truth ever reached the world. Yet if she hesitated, the evidence might vanish, swallowed by the very syndicate she sought to expose.

Her phone buzzed again, this time, a single text message.

It read: *"Nice find. Let's talk."*

No name. Only a location: an old tea stall near Shivajinagar.

Morning light crept reluctantly into Pune, but Avni felt no sense of comfort. The message still glowed on her phone screen: *"Nice find. Let's talk."* The tea stall in Shivajinagar was familiar to her, a modest place where rickshaw drivers gathered before dawn, where steam from boiling kettles mixed with the chatter of early commuters. It was public enough to provide cover, yet secluded enough for secrets to be exchanged.

Avni dressed cautiously, slipping the photograph and a copy of the notes into her bag while leaving the original box hidden under her bed. If this was a trap, she refused to hand everything over. Her recorder and pen were tucked in her jacket pocket, ready to capture every word.

By mid-morning, she arrived at the stall. The aroma of cardamom tea drifted through the air as rainwater trickled along the gutters. Customers came and went, their voices blending with the hiss of boiling milk. Avni chose a corner seat, her back against the wall, her eyes scanning every face.

Minutes stretched painfully. Then a man in his late fifties, wearing a neatly pressed kurta and carrying a walking stick, approached. His posture was frail, but his eyes were piercing. Without asking permission, he sat opposite her.

"You must be Avni," he said softly, his tone carrying the weight of recognition. "You've found what Vihaan left behind."

Avni's throat tightened. "Who are you?"

The man leaned closer, lowering his voice. "Once, I was part of it. The syndicate. But I left before they destroyed me too. And now, you hold the very thing they've been trying to erase for twenty years."

Avni leaned forward, her pen poised over her notebook though her pulse was hammering too loud for steady writing. The man sipped his tea slowly, as if choosing his words with surgical precision.

“My name won’t matter,” he began, eyes fixed on the steaming glass in his hand. “But once, I sat in meetings where matches were planned not on the field, but at tables like this one. Vihaan was the only one who stood against it. He was young, idealistic. They asked him to lose a match, just one. He refused.”

Avni’s fingers tightened around her pen. “And for that, they made him disappear?”

The man gave a bitter laugh. “Disappear is a polite word. They needed him gone, but not in a way that would raise suspicion. He was supposed to sign a contract that night. Instead, he left a clue… the bat, the engravings, the notebook. He thought someone would piece it together.” His eyes shifted to her bag knowingly.

“Who?” Avni pressed. “Who gave the order?”

The man’s expression darkened. “You already have the initials. A.T. for Tilekar, yes, but he wasn’t the mastermind. He tried to shield Vihaan and paid with his life. V.S., that one you must fear the most. Vikram Singh still runs their network. He’s untouchable, at least in daylight.”

Avni’s breath caught. The name wasn’t unfamiliar. Vikram Singh, the charismatic businessman who now sponsored half the cricket tournaments in Pune. A man praised in the media, yet whispered about in hushed tones.

The informant leaned closer. “If you intend to pursue this, understand: they’ll come for you. Just as they came for him.”

His words settled over her like smoke, warning, prophecy, and challenge all at once.

CHAPTER : 4

THE SYNDICATE'S SHADOW

Avni left the tea stall with her mind buzzing, every word of the old insider echoing in her head. *Vikram Singh.* The name now loomed over her investigation like a storm cloud. She had seen his face countless times on billboards and in glossy magazines, hailed as the man who revitalized cricket in Pune with his sponsorships, academies, and charitable foundations. To the public, he was a savior. But to those who whispered behind closed doors, he was something far darker.

As she walked along the crowded lanes of Shivajinagar, Avni opened her recorder and replayed the man's words. His confession was shaky, veiled in fear, but damning nonetheless. Still, it wasn't enough to publish. Allegations without proof would vanish into the wind, dismissed as conspiracy or character assassination. She needed documents, transactions, witnesses, something concrete to pierce Singh's carefully polished image.

Back at her flat, she pulled up Singh's profile on her laptop. His empire extended far beyond cricket: construction companies, real estate, betting syndicates disguised as “sports analytics firms.” The money trails twisted through shell corporations and offshore accounts. It was a labyrinth, deliberately designed to confuse anyone reckless enough to follow.

But what struck Avni most was Singh’s proximity to Vihaan’s final matches. Old press clippings showed Singh present at charity events, photographed with the young prodigy just weeks before his disappearance. His smile in those photos was wide, genuine even, but now, Avni saw it as something else. A mask.

She leaned back, staring at the ceiling. To confront Vikram Singh meant entering the lion’s den. And lions didn’t take kindly to trespassers.

Yet for the first time, the path ahead felt unmistakably clear.

The following day, Avni set herself up in a corner of a bustling café near Fergusson College Road. The chatter of students and the hiss of espresso machines provided a safe background hum, perfect for blending in. She spread her notes across the table, mapping Singh’s network like a spider web. His companies connected to event managers, betting platforms, and even player management firms. Each line she drew tightened the noose, yet each discovery made her feel the walls closing in.

She paused when she noticed something unsettling, two men seated by the window, pretending to read newspapers. Their gazes flicked toward her one too many times. She shifted her laptop screen, suddenly aware of how vulnerable she was in the open. Singh's reach wasn't abstract anymore; it was sitting twenty feet away, watching her.

Avni packed her things calmly, refusing to betray her alarm. She stepped outside into the afternoon sun, weaving through the crowd of college students and street vendors. For a moment, she thought she had shaken them. But as she turned onto a quieter lane, she caught the reflection in a shop window, one of the men was still behind her.

Her pulse surged. She quickened her pace, ducking into a side alley that spilled onto Jangli Maharaj Road. The crowd there gave her temporary cover. She slipped into a small bookstore, hiding between tall shelves of dusty volumes until the footsteps faded.

Breathing hard, Avni clutched her bag. This was confirmation. Singh's people knew she was onto something.

And if they were already tailing her, then the evidence she carried was far more dangerous than she had imagined.

Avni waited in the bookstore, her breath steadying as she pretended to skim the spine of a cricket biography. The air smelled faintly of old paper and incense from the nearby temple. Just as she was about to step back out, a low voice spoke from behind her.

"You shouldn't be walking alone with files like those."

She spun around, startled. A middle-aged man stood there, his hair flecked with gray, his eyes sharp yet weary. He wore a simple kurta and carried a cloth satchel slung across his shoulder.

"Who are you?" Avni demanded, her hand tightening around her bag strap.

"Someone who knows what Singh is capable of," the man replied. He glanced toward the doorway before continuing, "I worked for him once, long enough to understand the way he destroys anyone who threatens his empire."

Avni studied him carefully. His tone carried neither bravado nor threat, only a bitter resignation. "If that's true, why talk to me? Why now?"

He sighed, lowering his gaze. "Because I've seen too many people silenced. Coaches, players, even journalists. Singh's power lies in fear. But fear doesn't protect forever. You're stirring things up, and that might give me a chance to atone."

The man introduced himself as Raghav Deshmukh, a former fixer who had arranged deals for Singh during the early 2000s. His knowledge of hidden accounts and secret meetings could blow open doors Avni hadn't even reached yet.

But trust was a fragile currency.

"How do I know you're not leading me into a trap?" she asked quietly.

Raghav's lips curved into a faint, tired smile. "You don't. But if you walk away now, Singh wins again."

Avni reluctantly agreed to hear him out, choosing a secluded corner inside the bookstore. The owner, an elderly man reading a Marathi newspaper at the counter, barely noticed them as Raghav leaned closer, lowering his voice to a conspiratorial whisper.

"Singh's empire isn't just betting slips and whispered odds," Raghav began. "It's layered. First are the small-time bookies who operate around stadiums. They funnel money upward to middlemen who manage accounts through offshore companies. But the true control rests with Singh and a circle of board members who protect him."

Avni scribbled notes furiously, though her hand trembled. "Are you saying the cricket board itself shields him?"

Raghav nodded grimly. "Not all, but enough. Officials who profit from match outcomes, politicians who receive cuts, even players who look the other way. It's not just corruption, it's a machinery built to appear legitimate."

He took a deep breath, his eyes clouded by memory. "I've sat in hotel suites where matches were priced before a ball was bowled. I've carried envelopes stuffed with cash to umpires. I've seen careers destroyed when players refused to comply."

Avni felt her throat tighten. The scale of it was larger than she had ever imagined. “And Vihaan Palkar?” she asked softly.

Raghav hesitated, then leaned back, scanning the shelves as if the books themselves might betray him. “Vihaan was different. He didn’t bend. Singh wanted him to throw a semi-final for millions. Vihaan refused, and that refusal cost him everything.”

The words struck Avni like a thunderclap. The story she was chasing wasn’t just about fixing, it was about a man who vanished because he chose integrity over compromise.

Raghav’s voice lowered further, the weight of his confession pressing into every syllable. “The night Vihaan disappeared, there was a meeting at the Blue Orchid Hotel on Bund Garden Road. Singh had summoned him. I was there, not in the room, but waiting outside with the others. Vihaan walked in, carrying his kit bag and that bat of his, the one everyone said had magic in it. He looked calm, determined. But there was fire in his eyes.”

Avni leaned forward, her heart pounding. “What happened inside?”

Raghav shook his head slowly. “I never heard the words, but I saw the aftermath. Voices were raised. Singh stormed out first, red with rage, shouting into his phone. Vihaan didn’t come out at all. When I went back the next morning, the hotel staff said the room had been cleared, his belongings gone. Officially, it was as if he had never checked in."

Avni's chest tightened. "So he was taken? Silenced?"

Raghav exhaled sharply. "All I know is that Singh ordered me to dispose of a duffel bag later that night. It was heavy, wrapped in cloth. I never opened it, but I've lived with the question of what was inside for twenty years." His eyes clouded with guilt.

The café's distant chatter seemed to vanish; Avni heard only her own heartbeat. This wasn't speculation anymore, this was testimony.

She swallowed hard. "If what you're saying is true, Raghav, then Vihaan's disappearance wasn't just tragedy. It was murder."

Raghav's face tightened. "Call it whatever you want. But if you pursue this, Singh won't let you live to print it."

Avni sat in silence for a long moment, staring at the scuffed floorboards of the bookstore. Every instinct in her screamed caution. Raghav might be sincere, or he might be a lure, bait to drag her straight into Singh's trap. The weight of that uncertainty pressed on her chest like a stone.

Finally, she raised her eyes, meeting his steady gaze. "If I trust you, it could cost me everything. If I don't, I may never uncover what happened to Vihaan."

Raghav gave a bitter chuckle. “That’s the same choice he faced, Ms. Mhatre. The only difference is, you still have time to walk away.”

The words lingered, unsettling her. She remembered the kids who had found the bat, their innocent curiosity. She thought of Vihaan’s century that the world still remembered, of the headlines that should have celebrated a career but instead marked his vanishing. She couldn’t walk away, not now.

“Fine,” she said firmly. “But if you betray me, Raghav, I’ll make sure the whole city knows your face before Singh can bury the story.”

His expression flickered with something between respect and sorrow. “Fair enough.”

Avni pulled out her phone and slid it across the table. “Prove your worth. Names, dates, accounts, something I can verify. Without that, you’re just another ghost story.”

Raghav tapped his satchel, then unzipped it slowly. From inside, he drew a thin folder bound with a rubber band. The papers were yellowed, corners frayed, but the typed print and handwritten notes spoke of records not meant to survive.

He placed it gently between them. “Here’s where the shadows begin.”

Avni untied the rubber band with careful fingers, as though the folder itself might detonate. The first few pages were faded bank receipts, stamped with foreign symbols. Offshore accounts, she recognized the names of tax havens whispered in investigative circles: Mauritius, Cayman Islands, even accounts routed through Singapore. The amounts staggered her, millions transferred in tidy increments, concealed under the names of shell corporations.

Her eyes moved to the handwritten annotations in the margins. Beside one transfer, a note scrawled in hurried Marathi: *"For stadium renovation, Pune."* She frowned. The figures were astronomical, far more than any legitimate construction budget.

Raghav leaned closer. "That's one of Singh's oldest tricks. Money disguised as infrastructure funding. The stadium never saw a rupee of it, but officials lined their pockets."

Avni flipped another sheet and froze. This time, names appeared, initials at first, then full signatures. A board member from the Maharashtra Cricket Association. A former state selector. Even a politician from Shivajinagar, who often appeared in cricket fundraisers. Each name carried the weight of betrayal.

Her pen scratched furiously across her notepad. Every revelation widened the circle of complicity, tying Singh not only to betting but to the very guardians of the sport.

She glanced at Raghav. "If these documents are genuine, this isn't just a syndicate. It's a network rooted in Pune's cricketing foundation."

Raghav's jaw tightened. "Exactly. Singh doesn't just fix matches. He fixes the system itself. That's why nobody touches him."

Avni swallowed, the weight of the folder heavy in her lap. This wasn't a story anymore, it was a war.

Avni turned another page, and her pulse quickened. Amidst the financial records lay a thin sheet of ruled paper, covered with odd notations, letters, numbers, and dates that seemed out of place. She tilted her head, scanning the code. One date leapt out at her: *15 March, 2005*.

Her breath caught. That was the exact day of Vihaan Palkar's last recorded match.

"Why is this here?" she whispered.

Raghav's expression darkened. "Those aren't just numbers. It's how Singh's men tracked manipulated games. Each entry corresponds to overs, runs, and outcomes they prearranged. That date, Vihaan's century, was supposed to be fixed. Only, he refused."

Avni studied the page more closely. Alongside the date was an entry marked *'P-100'*, circled twice in red ink. "What does this mean?"

Raghav hesitated. "It meant a guarantee. Singh expected Vihaan to stall at ninety-nine, to stop short of the record. A signal to bettors worldwide. But Vihaan hit a hundred anyway, and in that single stroke, he humiliated the syndicate. Millions were lost."

A chill rippled through Avni. The bat buried near the pavilion, the engraved initials, the sudden disappearance, everything tied back to this night. Vihaan hadn't vanished by chance; he had drawn a line Singh couldn't tolerate.

Avni traced the inked circle with her fingertip. "He left a clue. The bat wasn't just nostalgia, it was evidence."

Raghav's eyes narrowed. "And now you're holding the rest of it. But understand this, Avni: once Singh knows you've seen these papers, he won't stop until you're erased like Vihaan."

Avni closed the folder slowly, her hands trembling despite her efforts to appear composed. The paper inside felt like dynamite wrapped in manila, too volatile to keep, too dangerous to discard. She slid it back across the table toward Raghav.

"You keep it," she said cautiously. "If Singh's men are already tailing me, carrying this around would make me a moving target."

Raghav shook his head firmly. "No. They already know me. I'm a liability Singh tolerates only because I've stayed silent. But you, your voice still matters. If you vanish with these records, people will notice. That's your shield."

His words made sense, yet fear gnawed at her. Avni looked toward the glass door of the bookstore. The street outside was busy, but every passerby felt like a pair of eyes watching too closely.

She pressed her palm to the folder. "If I take this, I have to move carefully. No more cafés, no public meetings. Singh's men will strike when I least expect it."

Raghav's voice softened. "Then don't wait for them. Stay ahead. Hide the evidence somewhere safe. Work quietly. When the time comes, expose them in one strike."

Avni nodded slowly, her resolve hardening. She slipped the folder into her satchel, zipping it shut. The weight was almost unbearable, but it was also empowering. For the first time, she held proof that Vihaan's disappearance wasn't just rumor, it was conspiracy carved into numbers and ink.

Raghav leaned back, exhaling as though a burden had shifted from his shoulders. "Now, Ms. Mhatre, you're in the game. And once you're in, there's no walking away."

The bell above the bookstore door jingled, and Avni stiffened. Two men stepped inside, their movements too deliberate to be casual. One wore a leather jacket despite the humid Pune afternoon, the other carried a helmet under his arm, his eyes scanning the shelves with practiced sharpness.

Raghav's hand froze halfway to his satchel. He didn't need to speak; Avni knew instantly, they were Singh's men.

The shop owner barely looked up from his newspaper, but Avni could feel the change in the room, a tension as if the very air had been thickened. She hunched slightly, pulling her scarf higher over her head, pretending to be absorbed in a book.

The men moved deeper into the store, separating, their boots creaking against the wooden floor. One paused near the counter, flipping through magazines, while the other drifted toward the aisle where Avni stood. His footsteps were unhurried, predatory.

Raghav leaned closer, whispering without moving his lips. "Back exit. Left of the counter. Don't run until you're outside."

Avni's pulse hammered in her throat. She clutched her satchel tighter, feeling the folder press against her ribs. Every instinct screamed to flee, yet she forced herself to remain calm. She slid the book back onto the shelf, turned casually, and began walking toward the counter, her steps measured.

The man's gaze followed her, suspicion sharpening.

Just as she reached the counter, Raghav created a sudden distraction, he dropped his satchel, spilling papers across the floor. Both men turned instinctively.

Avni slipped behind the counter, pushed open the narrow wooden door, and vanished into the alley.

Her lungs burned with relief, but she knew escape was only temporary. Singh's shadow had already found her.

CHAPTER : 5

BENEATH THE FLOODLIGHTS

Night had fallen over Pune, the city lights twinkling like distant constellations. Avni moved cautiously along the empty streets, her satchel containing Raghav's folder pressing against her side. Every shadow seemed alive, every passing car a potential threat. She couldn't rely on cafés, bookstores, or familiar alleys anymore. Singh's reach was vast, and she was learning, painfully, that safety in public spaces was an illusion.

Her thoughts drifted back to the pavilion where the bat had been found and the notebook uncovered. That was where it had all begun, the first clue in a trail that led straight to Vihaan Palkar and, inevitably, to Vikram Singh. The abandoned stadiums, the floodlights, the silent terraces, they held answers, if she had the courage to look.

Avni arrived at a smaller, secondary ground in Pune used for practice matches. It was quiet, the floodlights off, the air thick with the smell of damp earth and old turf. She crouched behind a row of benches, surveying the pitch. The memory of Vihaan's last match, his century, the crowd's roar, the final strike that had defied the syndicate, played vividly in her mind.

She knelt at the edge of the field, brushing her fingers through the grass. Somewhere beneath it, hidden during that fateful night, there might still be a fragment of Vihaan's last attempt to leave a clue. The metal box, the bat, the notebook, all pieces of a puzzle no one had yet dared to assemble completely.

Her heart beat faster. This was no longer just investigation; it was a quest into the heart of a conspiracy that had festered for decades. And beneath the floodlights of an empty field, Avni felt the pulse of the past calling to her.

Avni drew a deep breath and lowered herself onto her knees at the edge of the pitch. The ground was damp, soft beneath her fingers, the earth cold in the night air. She reached into her bag for a small trowel, the same one she had used at the abandoned pavilion, and began scraping gently at the turf.

Her mind replayed Raghav's words: *"Look beneath the pitch."* This time, she understood it wasn't metaphorical. Vihaan had left something tangible, a message, proof, or both, hidden from the world that wanted to erase him.

Minutes passed. The rhythmic sound of scraping soil mingled with the distant hum of city traffic. Avni's muscles ached, but she persisted, guided by instinct and the fragments of knowledge she had pieced together. Finally, the trowel struck something hard.

Her breath caught. Brushing away the surrounding dirt revealed a small metal case, its edges corroded and corners dented. She tugged at it gently, lifting it free. It was heavier than expected, and as she carried it back to her satchel, she felt the weight of history pressing down on her.

Avni crouched on the grass, heart racing. She pried open the case carefully. Inside lay another notebook, smaller than the first, with Vihaan's handwriting scrawled across the pages. Schematics of field positions, cryptic notes about certain players, and a single sentence underlined multiple times: *"Trust no one, not even the familiar."*

The warning sent a chill down her spine. Vihaan had anticipated betrayal. Someone he had trusted had turned against him. And now, holding this notebook, Avni realized she had stepped into the same dangerous game.

Avni flipped open the notebook, her fingers trembling as she scanned Vihaan's handwriting. The lines were hurried, almost chaotic, yet each word was deliberate. Schemes of matches, initials of players, and subtle numerical codes littered the pages. It was like a language only someone familiar with cricket strategy, and betrayal, could decode.

Her eyes caught a recurring pattern. Certain matches were circled, accompanied by abbreviations: *"P.S., M.C.A., R.R."* At first, the letters seemed random, but Avni's journalist instincts clicked. They corresponded to board officials, selectors, and even regional clubs.

Vihaan had annotated which games were being manipulated, and who had a hand in each deception.

One page was marked with a bold red asterisk: *"March 14, Pune – Century. Don't miss."* She paused, heart racing. This was the night of Vihaan's final match, the one where he defied the syndicate by scoring a record-breaking century.

Beneath the date were coordinates, almost imperceptible, written in tiny numbers alongside a sketch of the stadium pitch. Avni squinted, realizing the markings weren't just positional, they indicated hidden compartments, secret locations where Vihaan had left clues for anyone brave enough to find them.

Her pulse quickened. If she followed this, she might uncover the full scope of what had happened the night Vihaan disappeared. But the risk was enormous. Singh's men were already tracking her, and now she held the very blueprint of Vihaan's defiance.

Avni clutched the notebook, the weight of its significance settling on her shoulders. Every step forward meant danger. Yet for the first time, she felt she was not merely chasing a story, she was following Vihaan's trail, walking the path he had tried to leave behind.

Avni left the pitch with careful, calculated steps, her satchel strapped tightly across her body. The night air of Pune was cool, yet the adrenaline coursing through her veins made her skin prick with tension. Every street corner, every flicker of light felt like it could conceal danger. Singh's reach was long, and she had to stay one step ahead.

Back in her apartment, she spread out Vihaan's notebook and Raghav's folder side by side. She compared the coded notes to the financial documents, tracing connections between manipulated matches and the people who had benefited. A clear pattern emerged: certain board officials, certain selectors, and a few prominent players had been involved repeatedly. Singh's control was methodical, precise, and merciless.

One set of coordinates drew her attention, a location near the outskirts of Pune, an abandoned storage warehouse once used to store cricket equipment. A faint sketch beside it indicated a hidden entrance beneath a loose floorboard. Her pulse quickened. Vihaan had deliberately left this clue, and it might hold the next piece of the puzzle.

Avni packed lightly: the notebook, folder, flashlight, gloves, and a small first-aid kit. She reviewed her plan, ensuring that no trace could lead Singh's men to her. Every step had to be calculated; mistakes were deadly.

Before leaving, she paused by the window, looking at the city sprawled below. Somewhere in Pune, the men of the syndicate were awake, watching, waiting. Yet, for the first time, Avni felt a strange determination. She wasn't just chasing Vihaan's story anymore, she was following his footsteps, treading the path he had left behind, hoping it would lead her to the truth.

The warehouse loomed at the edge of Pune's industrial district, a hulking silhouette against the faint glow of streetlights. Rust streaked the corrugated metal walls, and broken windows stared blankly at the empty road. Avni parked her scooter a few blocks away, the engine's hum swallowed by the night. She approached on foot, every sense alert.

The main entrance was locked, but Vihaan's sketch had indicated a side door partially hidden behind stacked crates. She pushed aside the wooden pallets and found it slightly ajar. A rush of stale air greeted her, carrying the scent of dust and forgotten equipment. The warehouse was a cavern of shadows, and every echo of her footsteps seemed amplified, bouncing off metal beams and concrete floors.

Avni knelt near the floor where the sketch indicated a hidden panel. The boards were loose, warped with age. With gloved hands, she carefully lifted the panel. Beneath it lay a small cavity, just large enough for a briefcase-sized container. Her breath hitched. This had to be another piece of Vihaan's trail.

As she tugged out the container, she noticed something else, a slip of paper pinned inside the cavity with a rusted nail. She pulled it free and unfolded it. Written in Vihaan's unmistakable handwriting was a short message: *"The truth is not in the open. Look where others fear to step."*

Avni swallowed hard. The cryptic note reinforced what she already knew: this journey would demand courage beyond ordinary limits. And with each step, Singh's shadow loomed closer, unseen but omnipresent.

She carefully stashed the container and note in her satchel, her resolve steeling. The next phase of the investigation had begun, and failure was not an option.

Avni settled into the shadows of a nearby alley and carefully opened the container. Inside were bundles of documents, some yellowed with age, others more recent, tied together with fraying string. Her eyes scanned quickly: letters, receipts, and handwritten notes, all meticulously organized.

One document immediately drew her attention, a ledger listing recent match outcomes alongside player initials and unusually high betting amounts. At the bottom was a name she recognized instantly: *R.K., a current cricket official.* Her stomach churned. The corruption was alive, ongoing, not confined to history. Singh's influence hadn't diminished; it had merely adapted, embedding itself in the present.

She flipped through more papers, uncovering photographs of discreet meetings, boardrooms, hotel lobbies, and private clubs. Faces she had seen in news articles and press conferences were captured exchanging envelopes, shaking hands, and signing documents. The photos formed a chilling tapestry: a living web of manipulation and deceit.

Avni's hands trembled as she realized the scope. This wasn't just Vihaan's story; it was evidence of an entire system designed to crush anyone who opposed it. And now she held the keys to exposing it.

Her phone vibrated, an unknown number. She hesitated, then answered cautiously.

A distorted voice spoke: "We know where you are. Leave the folder, or there will be consequences."

Avni's pulse raced, but she forced calm. Singh's men had found her trail, but she refused to surrender. She pocketed the documents, concealing them under layers of clothing.

The city around her seemed suddenly dangerous, every shadow a potential threat. Yet, in that moment, she understood one thing clearly: she could either let fear control her, or turn it into the resolve that would finally expose the truth.

Avni tucked the container and documents securely under her jacket and stepped out into the narrow alley. The street was deserted, but the hairs on her neck prickled. Footsteps echoed somewhere behind her, slow, deliberate, and unmistakably approaching.

She ducked behind a stack of crates, pressing her back against the cold concrete wall. Two men emerged from the shadows, scanning the area. Singh's operatives. They moved with purpose, confident that anyone foolish enough to be there alone would be an easy catch.

Avni held her breath, counting each step. The men paused near the warehouse entrance, speaking in low tones. One glanced in her direction, but she remained perfectly still, shadow blending with shadow. Seconds stretched like hours.

Then, a sudden idea sparked. Avni slipped into a narrow side passage, barely wide enough for her to squeeze through. The men heard the rustle but, assuming it was an animal or the wind, turned back. She forced herself to move silently, feet skimming the wet pavement, heart pounding.

She rounded the corner onto a quieter lane and paused to catch her breath. Her palms were slick with sweat. Each escape made her realize how close she was to being cornered. Singh's reach wasn't just a rumor, it was real, pervasive, and deadly.

Yet the notebook, the folder, and the container were still in her possession. Each item was proof, each item a weapon against the syndicate. Avni's mind raced, calculating her next move.

Tonight had been a test. And she had passed. But she knew the war was far from over. Singh's shadow loomed, and the chase had only just begun.

Avni navigated Pune's labyrinthine streets with careful precision, avoiding main roads and well-lit areas. Every passing motorbike or late-night pedestrian set her nerves on edge. She needed a safe space, a place to spread out the contents of the container without fear of intrusion.

Her apartment was risky. Even though she had been careful, Singh's operatives had already found her once. She settled on an old storage room she occasionally rented in Shivajinagar, ostensibly for document backups. It was quiet, isolated, and nondescript, a perfect hideout.

Once inside, she placed the container on a table and methodically emptied its contents. The folders, photographs, receipts, and letters were spread across the surface like a chaotic map. Avni's eyes scanned each page carefully. She recognized patterns linking current officials to past conspiracies, confirming that Singh's syndicate had been active for decades.

Among the documents was a thick envelope marked with the same red initials Vihaan had used in his notebook: *V.P.* Avni's hands trembled slightly as she opened it. Inside were photographs from the very night Vihaan disappeared, capturing key players in clandestine meetings. More chillingly, a set of letters detailed instructions for silencing anyone who threatened the syndicate, threats that had apparently been executed.

She leaned back in her chair, her mind racing. The scope of corruption was breathtaking, the danger palpable. Every signature, every photo, every note she now possessed was proof of a conspiracy that could shake Pune's cricketing world to its core.

Avni realized that from this small room, armed with evidence and determination, she had the power to expose the truth. But she also understood the stakes: one wrong move, and Singh's men would be there before dawn.

Avni spread the photographs and documents in front of her like a detective mapping a crime scene. Each image, each note, each ledger entry was a thread in a tangled web of deception. She began connecting the dots, officials, players, and promoters who had benefited from manipulated matches. The pattern was unmistakable.

One photograph drew her attention: a group of board officials laughing in a hotel lobby, envelopes exchanged surreptitiously. The timestamp was the night of Vihaan's last match. Nearby, another image showed the same men entering a private suite with an unidentified courier. The ledger in the container listed large sums that corresponded precisely to these events.

Avni's fingers traced the lines between names and numbers. Every match that had been supposedly "fixed" appeared in Vihaan's notebook, annotated with subtle notes only an insider could understand. She realized that Vihaan had been documenting the entire network, leaving behind clues for someone brave enough to follow.

Her pulse quickened as she cross-referenced the financial records with current events. It was not just history, many of these people still held power in Pune's cricketing world. If she published this, it wouldn't just expose Singh; it would shake the foundations of the city's entire sporting structure.

Avni paused, looking at the red initials Vihaan had used repeatedly: *V.S.* Vikram Singh. Every path she traced ultimately led back to him. The realization hit like a thunderclap: Singh wasn't just a figurehead; he was the architect, the lynchpin controlling the syndicate from shadows.

Her resolve hardened. Evidence was in her hands, danger close at every corner, and time slipping away. The choice was clear, she would pursue the truth, no matter the risk.

Avni leaned back in her chair, her eyes scanning the array of evidence before her. The photographs, ledgers, and Vihaan's notes formed a map of deception, betrayal, and greed. She needed a plan, rushed action would mean disaster. Singh's men were relentless, and any slip could cost her everything.

She grabbed her notebook and began outlining her strategy. First, verify the authenticity of key documents. Cross-check the signatures and financial trails. Next, identify whistle-blowers still alive, insiders willing to speak under anonymity. Finally, locate a safe method to release the story without alerting Singh prematurely.

Her mind replayed Raghav's warnings: *"Stay ahead. Move quietly. Timing is everything."* She knew she couldn't do this alone. There were too many moving pieces, too many eyes watching. Vihaan had tried to leave breadcrumbs, but even his clues carried immense danger.

Avni paused at one photograph, a close-up of Singh with a group of officials at a charity event. The same photo appeared in the ledger notes with an arrow pointing to an envelope on the table. That envelope, she realized, might hold tangible evidence, names, bank transfers, contracts, proof of Singh's direct involvement. If she could locate it, she would have the leverage needed to expose the network completely.

Her fingers tightened around the pen. The night outside was quiet, deceptive in its calm. Singh's operatives were out there, but so was opportunity. The map of corruption was now laid bare on her table, and Avni understood that with careful planning, patience, and courage, she could turn the tide.

The notebook and folder weren't just evidence, they were weapons. And beneath the floodlights of Pune's cricketing world, Avni resolved to wield them with precision.

CHAPTER : 6

THE CHARITY GAMBIT

The morning sun filtered weakly through Pune's hazy skyline as Avni reviewed her plan. The charity event was the next key target. Singh always maintained a polished public image, masking the ruthless operator behind it. If she could infiltrate the event, even discreetly, she might gather proof of his ongoing operations and link them to the decades-old syndicate Vihaan had documented.

Avni dressed conservatively, blending in with the philanthropic crowd, silk scarves, muted jewelry, and a notebook concealed under her handbag. The event was being held at a grand heritage hall in central Pune, its marble floors and ornate chandeliers creating an air of sophistication. Socialites, board officials, and journalists milled about, unaware of the storm that was about to descend.

She scanned the guest list, noting familiar names from Vihaan's notebook. Several officials she had identified as complicit in match-fixing were slated to attend, along with players whose careers had mysteriously flourished. Singh himself would arrive later in the evening, always the star of the spectacle, smiling for the cameras, shaking hands, donating checks for causes that obscured his darker dealings.

Avni moved cautiously among the crowd, her camera discreetly tucked under her arm. Her goal was simple: observe, document, and identify connections. Every handshake, every whispered conversation, could be a lead. Every glance or sudden movement might betray a secret.

She paused by a small table of envelopes and invitations, her mind returning to Vihaan's notes. The clues he had left were guiding her, step by careful step. The charity gala was not just a social affair, it was the stage where Singh's influence could be traced, and potentially, exposed.

The game had entered a new arena, and Avni was ready to play.

Avni moved through the gala carefully, blending into groups of well-dressed attendees while keeping a close eye on interactions. At first, the event seemed innocuous, glasses clinked, polite laughter echoed, and cameras flashed for social media coverage. But she had learned to look beneath the surface.

Near a corner of the hall, she noticed a cluster of officials exchanging envelopes with quiet, precise gestures. The subtlety of the exchange suggested that the contents were more than mere donations. Avni ducked behind a pillar, raising her camera just enough to capture photographs without attracting attention. Each image was a potential breadcrumb linking back to Singh's network.

A waiter passed with a silver tray, concealing slips of paper tucked beneath cocktail napkins. Avni noted the recipients: a few familiar names from Vihaan's notebook. Their interactions were too synchronized to be random. She scribbled quick notes, heart racing as realization struck. These seemingly ordinary events were carefully choreographed covers for illicit transactions.

From the far end of the hall, Singh arrived, impeccably dressed and smiling, his charisma drawing immediate attention. He shook hands, posed for photos, and accepted applause for his "charitable contributions." Yet Avni noticed subtle signs: the slight nod to an aide, the fleeting exchange of envelopes, and the hurried glances between board members. Each motion reinforced what Vihaan's notes had suggested, Singh's influence was omnipresent, his control total.

Avni exhaled slowly, reminding herself to remain patient. Capturing a single misstep, a single unguarded act, could unravel the web of deception he had carefully spun. The night was young, and the game of shadows was only just beginning.

Avni's eyes locked onto a discreet corner of the hall where Singh had moved, flanked by two of his closest aides. A senior board official approached, sliding an envelope into Singh's hand with the ease of routine. Singh didn't just accept it; he glanced around the hall, ensuring no one else noticed, and then whispered something to the aide beside him.

The subtlety of the exchange made her pulse race. This was the direct proof she needed, correspondence linking Singh to financial transactions tied to ongoing match manipulations. Avni adjusted her camera lens, zooming in while pretending to check her notes. Every movement was measured, every click nearly silent in the hushed elegance of the hall.

Nearby, a player known for sudden spikes in performance hesitated near the same official, receiving a folded note. The pattern was unmistakable. The hierarchy of control was being enacted before her eyes: envelopes, nods, and secret instructions. It was a ritual of corruption, hidden under the guise of charity and civility.

Avni scribbled furiously in her notebook, matching names, dates, and positions to Vihaan's coded notes. Every detail reinforced the dangerous truth: Singh was not merely a relic of the past; he was actively orchestrating manipulation in the present.

A faint chill ran down her spine. She realized the room could be watched, cameras might be planted, and any sudden movement could expose her. Yet the potential payoff was too great to ignore.

Carefully, Avni documented each exchange, committing names, gestures, and timings to memory. She understood that these photographs and notes could finally provide the undeniable bridge between Vihaan's disappearance and the continuing syndicate operations.

Tonight, the threads of history and present converged. Singh's web was visible, and Avni was in the center of it.

Avni felt the weight of her satchel pressing against her side, reminding her that the folder and notebook were still concealed beneath her coat. Every step had to be measured; one misstep, and Singh's men would spot her. She scanned the room again, noting the positions of the aides and officials she had documented. Timing was crucial.

The music from the orchestra masked her footsteps as she edged toward the exit, blending with groups of guests moving to the dining area. Her eyes flicked to Singh, who was now engaged in animated conversation with a politician from her list. Every handshake, every smile, concealed the undercurrent of collusion she had just captured on camera.

Near the exit, a waiter passed carrying trays of hors d'oeuvres. Avni used the distraction, moving behind him and letting the crowd obscure her retreat. A bead of sweat trickled down her temple as she silently calculated the distance to her scooter parked a few blocks away.

Once outside, she didn't pause. Pune's streets were quiet, shadows stretching across the pavement, offering both concealment and risk. She navigated through back alleys, keeping the container, folder, and notebook tightly against her chest. Every glance over her shoulder made her heart leap, but there was no sign of pursuit, for now.

Finally, she reached the small café she sometimes used as a temporary hideout. Locking the door behind her, Avni exhaled deeply. The night had been perilous, but she now possessed undeniable evidence linking Singh to ongoing corruption.

As she spread out the materials once more, Avni understood the stakes: exposing Singh meant challenging a network that had existed for decades. Yet the evidence in her hands offered a single path forward, truth, finally illuminated beneath the shadows of deceit.

Avni spread the photographs, notebooks, and ledgers across the café table, her fingers tracing the connections she had observed. Each piece of evidence reinforced the network Vihaan had documented: envelopes exchanged, handshakes performed with precision, and subtle nods that signaled silent obedience. The syndicate's web extended from past matches to the present, entangling officials, players, and politicians alike.

She began categorizing the materials. One stack contained photographs, each annotated with names, dates, and locations. Another held financial records, meticulously marked to indicate suspicious transfers. A third comprised Vihaan's notes, full of cryptic codes and sketches that now made more sense in context.

Avni paused at a particularly telling photograph: Singh accepting an envelope from a senior board official while glancing around as if ensuring no one noticed. The same official appeared in Vihaan's notebook, annotated as a key collaborator in match-fixing. The clarity was chilling,

Singh had orchestrated these manipulations personally, extending his influence into every corner of the cricketing world.

Her pen scratched furiously across her notebook as she charted a plan. First, she needed to cross-reference the photographs with financial records to create an unbroken chain of proof. Next, she would identify insiders willing to corroborate her findings. Finally, she would prepare to release the story strategically, ensuring maximum exposure while minimizing personal risk.

Avni leaned back, exhaling slowly. The enormity of what she held pressed against her chest, but it also fueled her determination. Vihaan had left a trail, and she was now following it to its end. Tonight, the pieces of a decades-old puzzle were coming together, and Singh's carefully constructed empire was beginning to appear vulnerable under the relentless scrutiny of truth.

Avni leaned over her notes, her mind racing as she drafted discreet messages to potential insiders. Each contact had to be approached carefully, any hint of exposure could result in silence, or worse. She used encrypted emails and burner phone numbers, layering her communications with plausible deniability.

Her first attempt was a former stadium manager, someone who had been mentioned in Vihaan's notebook and had likely witnessed irregularities during matches. Avni's fingers hovered over the keyboard, crafting a message that was urgent yet noncommittal: *"I have information about long-standing irregularities in Pune cricket. If you are willing to talk discreetly, reply to this number. Trust is essential."*

Next, she targeted a retired player known for integrity, whose name appeared in Vihaan's annotations. The message needed to convey the gravity of the situation without revealing her sources or the full scope of her findings. One wrong word could tip off Singh's network.

Avni paused, glancing at the pile of documents on the table. The photographs, ledgers, and notebooks collectively formed a web of corruption that stretched decades deep. She realized that these contacts were not just sources, they were potential allies in bringing the syndicate to justice.

Her phone buzzed. A reply from the retired player appeared, cautious but willing: *"We can meet. Safe location. Tomorrow. No electronic devices."*

Avni allowed herself a brief moment of relief. A single ally could make a difference, and this was the first tangible step in mobilizing support.

Yet, she knew the dangers remained. Singh's operatives were still active, watching, waiting. Every attempt to expose the truth brought her closer to confrontation, but also closer to justice.

Avni gathered the materials, double-checking her security protocols, preparing for the next phase of the investigation.

Avni spent the evening planning meticulously. The meeting with the retired player was scheduled for early morning in a discreet tea shop on the outskirts of Pune. She mapped multiple escape routes, noting alleys, side streets, and parked vehicles that could serve as temporary cover. Singh's operatives could strike at any moment, and caution was her only ally.

She packed her essentials: the notebook, folder, and container, each concealed in separate compartments of her bag. A small flashlight, gloves, and a burner phone completed her kit. Avni rehearsed mental scenarios, imagining every possible outcome, from a straightforward discussion to an ambush orchestrated by Singh's men.

The retired player's response had been cautious, but hopeful. His willingness to meet indicated he understood the risk, yet trusted her enough to come forward. Avni reminded herself that alliances in this investigation were fragile; one wrong move could shatter the fragile trust she was cultivating.

She reviewed the evidence one more time, connecting dots between the photographs, financial records, and Vihaan's coded notes. Patterns emerged, revealing not just the structure of the syndicate, but its methodical approach to silencing opposition. Each piece of paper was a potential weapon, if presented correctly, it could topple Singh's empire.

Night deepened over Pune, the streets quiet except for distant traffic. Avni's mind raced, balancing strategy with survival. The next twenty-four hours could determine the course of the investigation, and perhaps, her own fate.

Clutching her bag tightly, she closed her eyes briefly, centering herself. Determination replaced anxiety. The game had shifted from observation to action. Tomorrow, she would confront history, confront Singh's legacy, and move one step closer to exposing the truth buried beneath decades of deception.

Dawn was breaking over Pune as Avni approached the tea shop. The streets were quiet, bathed in the soft gold of early morning, yet every step felt charged with tension. She kept to the shadows, her satchel secured across her body, eyes scanning for any unusual movement. Singh's operatives could be anywhere, and she assumed they were already on alert after the charity gala.

The tea shop was small and unassuming, its wooden sign swaying slightly in the morning breeze. Avni paused at the entrance, observing the surroundings. A few early customers sipped their tea, and a delivery man stacked crates at the back, mundane activity, yet every ordinary detail could conceal danger.

She slipped inside, choosing a table near the back, facing the door. Her eyes darted to every corner, noting possible exits and cover points. Minutes felt like hours. The retired player was due any moment, and Avni had to maintain vigilance without appearing paranoid.

Finally, a man in his late fifties entered, moving with cautious grace. He scanned the room before settling into the chair across from her. Avni recognized him immediately, his demeanor calm, but his eyes sharp, carrying the weight of someone who had witnessed decades of corruption.

They exchanged cautious greetings. No phones, no unnecessary gestures. The man leaned forward, whispering: "I know why you're here. Vihaan… he trusted no one, but he left a trail. You need to follow it carefully. Singh will not forgive mistakes."

Avni nodded, absorbing his words. This was more than a meeting; it was a gateway into the syndicate's inner workings. Every detail he provided could be the key to exposing the conspiracy, and every misstep could be fatal.

The retired player leaned closer, his voice low and deliberate. "Singh's influence extends far beyond what most see. Board officials, players, and even some journalists, they all operate under his direction. Every match he manipulates is a demonstration of power."

Avni scribbled notes quickly, her eyes flicking between him and the door. "Do you have proof? Something I can document?" she asked.

He hesitated, glancing around before sliding a folded envelope across the table. "These are internal memos and payment schedules. They link directly to manipulated matches over the past five years. Cross-reference them with Vihaan's notes, he foresaw this, predicted patterns, and left instructions for anyone capable of connecting the dots."

Avni's hands trembled slightly as she opened the envelope. Inside were letters, unsigned but clearly authorized, detailing player selections, match strategies, and financial incentives disguised as bonuses. Every document confirmed what Vihaan had documented decades ago, the syndicate wasn't a relic; it was thriving, adapting, and ruthless.

The retired player continued, "If Singh suspects you have these, you're already a target. He watches carefully. You must move cautiously, verify every source, and never act alone. One wrong step, and the trail ends with you."

Avni nodded, determination hardening in her chest. She realized that this was more than an investigation, it was a battle against a system designed to protect itself at all costs. Every shred of evidence she possessed could topple the syndicate, but only if wielded with precision.

The café felt smaller, the walls closing in as the weight of responsibility settled on her shoulders. This was the turning point: with the insider's help and Vihaan's trail, Avni had the opportunity to expose Singh's empire, but danger shadowed every move.

Avni folded the envelope carefully, slipping it into a hidden compartment in her satchel. She kept her posture relaxed, casual, though every muscle in her body remained alert. Singh's operatives could strike at any moment, and she couldn't afford even a single misstep.

The retired player gave her a final nod. "Remember, you're not just carrying evidence. You're carrying responsibility. Every document, every photograph could expose decades of corruption, but it also paints a target on your back. Move cautiously."

Avni acknowledged him silently. She had learned the lesson the hard way: in this city, truth came with a price. She needed to exit carefully, retrace her path, and ensure no one had followed her.

She rose, keeping her movements smooth, and scanned the café once more. Other patrons remained oblivious, sipping their morning tea, unaware of the web of deceit being unraveled at the back table. Avni took a deep breath, slipping her hands into her pockets as she prepared to leave.

Outside, the early morning streets of Pune were quieter than usual, the air crisp with the first rays of sunlight. Avni stuck to side streets, doubling back where possible to mislead any potential followers. Her mind raced with strategy: secure the documents at a safe location, cross-reference the materials, and identify the next layer of the syndicate's operations.

By the time she reached a hidden lane leading to a safe house, the sense of danger had not diminished. If anything, it had intensified. Every step forward brought her closer to the truth, and closer to the people who would stop at nothing to keep it buried.

Avni paused, looking back over her shoulder. The city seemed peaceful, but she knew better. Singh's shadow was everywhere. She tightened her grip on the satchel and moved on, ready for the next phase of the hunt.

CHAPTER : 7

- - - - - - - - - - - -

THREADS OF DECEPTION

The safe house was small, nondescript, tucked into a quiet lane in Pune. Avni entered cautiously, double-checking the lock behind her. Inside, the air was still, heavy with the scent of old paper and coffee. She spread the contents of the envelope and the container across the table, methodically arranging photographs, letters, ledgers, and Vihaan's notebook.

Her eyes scanned the documents, connecting names, dates, and transactions. Singh's network was sprawling, intricate, and ruthless, yet patterns emerged. The same officials and players recurred, always in positions to benefit from manipulated matches. Each photograph corroborated a note from Vihaan's notebook; every letter aligned with the financial ledgers. The conspiracy, decades in the making, was fully visible in front of her.

Avni paused at a page in Vihaan's notebook, the coded handwriting suddenly clear in light of the insider's documents. Circles, arrows, and initials all pointed to strategic interventions in matches, orchestrated by Singh's allies. The letters from the envelope revealed the mechanics of bribes, performance incentives, and deliberate silencing of dissenting players.

She realized that the documents not only confirmed historical corruption but also exposed ongoing operations. Singh had modernized the syndicate, leveraging influence, intimidation, and financial manipulation to maintain absolute control. Each revelation tightened the knot of danger around her, one mistake could lead to discovery, and the consequences would be severe.

Avni leaned back, rubbing her temples. The sheer magnitude of the conspiracy was daunting, but clarity brought purpose. She had the evidence, the trail, and a potential ally in the retired player. Now, the challenge was strategic: how to unravel Singh's empire without triggering immediate retaliation.

Her pulse quickened. The game was no longer about observation, it was about action.

Avni cleared a space on the table and began laying out a chronological timeline of Singh's operations. Each document, photograph, and ledger entry became a marker, a puzzle piece slotting into a larger picture of manipulation and greed. She started with Vihaan's disappearance, tracing back to his last matches and the suspicious events noted in his coded journal.

Next, she added the charity gala evidence and the letters from the retired player. Dates, amounts, and recipient initials were carefully aligned with match schedules, board meetings, and player selections. Slowly, a pattern emerged: Singh had systematically infiltrated every level of the cricketing hierarchy. Board officials, team selectors, and even prominent players were complicit, directly or indirectly, in fixing matches, controlling careers, and eliminating threats.

Avni paused at a particularly revealing photograph showing Singh with an envelope in hand, a junior official leaning in discreetly. She annotated it, cross-referencing the ledger that confirmed a large transaction that same night. Each entry strengthened the chain of evidence, reducing gaps, and making the syndicate's network undeniable.

She worked methodically, noting inconsistencies and anomalies that might otherwise be dismissed. Each coded note from Vihaan now had context, an encrypted message that, when decoded, revealed instructions for whistleblowers, warnings about corrupt officials, and even hints about secret locations where critical evidence had been hidden.

Hours passed, and Avni's timeline began to resemble a map of Singh's empire, meticulous, ruthless, and chillingly precise. The weight of the discovery pressed down on her shoulders, but with it came a sense of purpose. She now had a clear strategy: identify the most vulnerable nodes in Singh's network and strike decisively, using Vihaan's trail as her guide.

The pieces were coming together. The next move would be critical.

Avni studied the timeline until the ink blurred. She needed a fulcrum, a single weak link she could pry open to topple a larger section of Singh's web. Among the names that kept resurfacing, one initial had appeared in ledgers and memos with unsettling regularity: R.K. The documents hinted at R.K.'s role in authorizing transfers and rubber- stamping inflated invoices. If she could place a credible face to those initials, she might find someone who'd rather talk than go to prison.

Cross- checking public filings and match rosters, Avni narrowed the field. R.K. matched a mid- level official, Rakesh Kothari, a paperwork- driven man who handled accounts for the Maharashtra Cricket Association. He wasn't glamorous. He liked his routines, his tea at the same stall, his predictable commute. Power lived above him; fear lived beneath it. That pattern made him vulnerable.

Her plan formed in cold, pragmatic strokes. She would not ambush Rakesh with a folder and a demand. She would test him. First: verify his involvement via small corroborations, two independent receipts from different banks, a photograph of Rakesh at a charity event annotated in Vihaan's notes, and a ledger entry that matched his approval stamp. Second: approach him not as accuser but as mirror, show him incontrovertible proof that he could be sacrificed to protect others unless he chose differently.

Avni also weighed Jamkar's role. The inspector had been ambiguous, guardian and threat in the same breath. For now, she would keep Jamkar informed only enough to be useful; full disclosure could cost her any advantage. Instead she prepared a low- risk meeting plan: neutral public place, burner phone, recorder hidden in a pen, and a contingency escape route.

She folded her notes, feeling the familiar surge, equal parts fear and focus. A single conversation with the right person, handled correctly, could crack the façade. She would make that call tonight.

Avni waited until late, when Pune's streets hummed with the last commuters and streetlights threw long shadows. She used a burner phone, clean, unlinked, and composed a terse message to Rakesh Kothari: *"I have documents you should see. If you value discretion, meet me at Laxmi Tea Stall, 7:30 a.m. No phones."* She did not hint at names or consequences. Fear, she knew, could be a lever; curiosity, another.

Sleep eluded her. She rehearsed the meeting in the hollow of the night, how to open the conversation gently, how to present proof incrementally, how to coax rather than coerce. She prepared a small packet: two photocopies of receipts, a cropped photograph showing R.K.'s signature next to a ledger sum, and a single, unambiguous bank transfer highlighted in red. Enough to startle, not enough to destroy instantly. If Rakesh blinked, she would press; if he froze, she would retreat.

Morning arrived humid and heavy. Avni chose plain clothes, a cotton kurta and simple sandals, and left the folder locked in the safe room. She carried only the packet and a recorder disguised as a pen. At 7:10 a.m., she took a seat at the tea stall, facing the entrance, watching faces, watching posture, cataloging habits. The world moved in small, revealing rituals: vendors arranging cups, a scooter's chain clinking, a man wiping yesterday's chalk off a menu board.

At 7:28, a middle- aged man approached cautiously, scanning the patrons. Rakesh Kothari had the posture she expected, careful, habitual. He sat two chairs away, ordered tea without looking at the vendor, and then, with deliberate slowness, turned his head as if rehearsing a decision.

Avni breathed and let the moment coagulate. This conversation would determine whether a single thread could become a knife through Singh's armor, or whether the armor would simply close tighter. She pushed the packet across the table and said, softly, "Look at this. No judgment. Just the choice."

Rakesh's hand hovered over the packet as if it might burn him. He unfolded the first photocopy with fingers that trembled more from habit than fear, accountant's precision undercut by sudden alarm. Avni watched every microexpression: the way his jaw tightened, the small gulp that betrayed his attempt at composure.

"This, this is from my desk," he whispered, voice barely audible over the clink of teacups. "Where did you get this?"

"Doesn't matter," Avni said evenly. "What matters is that it ties you to transfers signed off the night of the Pune charity event. You approved invoices that routed funds through shell firms. Your stamp is on them." She kept her tone low, non accusatory; accusation would make him retreat. “You don’t have to deny it. You can help now, or be pushed into becoming a scapegoat later.”

Rakesh stared at the paper as if it were an accusation and a lifeline at once. The lines on his face deepened. “If they find out I spoke…..” he began. Then he cut himself off, eyes darting to the street as if someone might be listening through the corrugated walls.

Avni slid the recorder- pen toward him, fingers brushing his. “If you talk, there are ways to protect you. Anonymity at first. Corroboration. Proof we can use in court. But we need names attached to the shell accounts, the wire routing, who gave the instructions. You sign a few forms, point to the emails, and the picture clears.”

Silence stretched. Finally, Rakesh exhaled, a sound like surrender. “There are emails,” he said at last, voice raw. “From an account, singhcorp.events@gmail.com, and directives came hidden in meeting minutes. I thought I was doing repairs to finance, not killing careers.” He looked up, terrified and repentant. “I can get you logs. But you have to promise… protection.”

Avni’s pen hovered. Promise was a word she could not guarantee absolutely. Still, she offered what she could: legal contacts, a neutral journalist who could vouch, and a staged path to safety if things went south. Rakesh nodded, the decision made. The first crack in Singh’s armor had widened.

Avni exhaled slowly, feeling the tension in her shoulders ease just enough to think clearly. Rakesh was willing to cooperate, but the information he held was volatile. She could not rush; one careless step, and both of them would become targets.

She instructed him quietly, "Send me one email at a time. Don't attach anything sensitive all at once. I'll confirm receipt, then we proceed to the next. Keep everything offline until then. Phones, notes, destroy duplicates." Rakesh nodded, his hands still shaking, eyes flicking to the street outside.

Avni reviewed the documents he had already described: emails embedded with coded instructions, meeting minutes annotated with initials of players and officials, and several receipts connecting Singh's shell companies to direct transfers for match outcomes. Each piece reinforced the timeline she had already been assembling, tightening the web of evidence so that it could not be dismissed as coincidence.

They spoke in hushed tones, careful not to draw attention from the café staff. Avni noted Rakesh's fear, he wasn't a hardened criminal; he was a man trapped in the machinery of corruption, now realizing the consequences of even minor compliance. That fear could be leveraged carefully to extract more precise data, but she would not push him too far.

By the time their conversation ended, a preliminary roadmap had emerged. Rakesh would provide digital logs, emails, and access to archived meeting minutes over the next week. In return, Avni offered guidance on how to navigate exposure safely.

As they parted, Avni's mind was already racing ahead. This first victory was critical, but it was only the beginning. Singh's network was vast, and each subsequent move would demand precision, patience, and unflinching courage.

The first crack had appeared in the syndicate's armor and Avni intended to widen it relentlessly.

Back in the safe house, Avni spread the first set of emails and meeting logs Rakesh had provided across the table. The subject lines were mundane: *"Budget Approvals," "Player Rotation," "Charity Contributions."* But hidden within the attachments were directives, subtly worded, that determined outcomes of matches and manipulated player selections.

She highlighted recurring names: board officials, selectors, and players whose performances had inexplicably spiked. Each email contained coded instructions, often disguised as logistical notes for tournaments or sponsorship deals. Avni cross-referenced them against Vihaan's notebook. The patterns matched perfectly, every prediction, every annotation aligned with the digital evidence.

Her pulse quickened. The proof was no longer theoretical; it was tangible and undeniable. Singh's influence was pervasive, embedded in every corner of the cricketing hierarchy. Even casual observers, like fans or local journalists, were unknowingly witnessing the results of his manipulations.

Avni began constructing a visual chart, linking names, dates, transactions, and match outcomes. The network, once abstract and intimidating, now took the form of an intricate spiderweb with Singh at the center. Each line represented control, coercion, or complicity.

She paused at an email marked with an unusual timestamp: 3:17 a.m., a directive for a sudden player substitution the night before a critical match. Cross-referencing with Vihaan's notes revealed that this was the match he had refused to fix, the one that triggered his disappearance. A shiver ran down her spine.

Avni leaned back, rubbing her eyes. The timeline, emails, and notebook now formed a blueprint of corruption. The question was no longer *whether* Singh's empire could be exposed, but *how*. Each next step had to be calculated, strategic, and, above all, safe.

The hunt was on. Singh's world was mapped and Avni was ready to move.

Avni studied the visual chart she had constructed, her eyes tracing the connections with painstaking care. Each thread represented influence, manipulation, or coercion. Singh sat at the center, but the network radiated outward through multiple layers, board officials, selectors, players, and financiers. To dismantle it, she had to move methodically, one link at a time.

Her gaze settled on a recurring name: Anil Deshmukh, a junior selector whose decisions consistently aligned with Singh's directives. Unlike Rakesh, Anil had influence over player placements and match strategies, making him a key node in the syndicate's operations. If she could secure his cooperation or extract incriminating evidence, the chain would extend directly to the top.

Avni reviewed the supporting documents: emails from Singh's accounts, meeting minutes with cryptic notes, and Vihaan's observations. Anil appeared in almost every instance where player substitutions or match outcomes had been suspiciously favorable. His pattern was subtle, almost invisible to anyone who did not know what to look for, but to Avni, it was glaring.

She began formulating a cautious approach. Unlike Rakesh, Anil had ambition and ego; direct intimidation could backfire. Avni would need to appeal to his self-preservation, perhaps even hinting at the consequences if he were exposed while offering a controlled way to cooperate. Timing, location, and method of contact would be critical.

Avni's mind raced with contingencies: safe meeting points, pre-recorded evidence, burner communications, and escape routes. Each decision now carried immense weight, one wrong move, and she could lose the opportunity to bring Singh down, or worse, become a target herself.

The first crack in the syndicate had been made with Rakesh. Now, Avni prepared to widen it strategically, setting her sights on Anil, the next pivotal piece in Singh's empire.

Avni waited until late afternoon, choosing a time when Anil Deshmukh would likely be alone and less guarded. She scouted potential meeting spots near his office and identified a quiet café tucked into a side street, neutral territory, with multiple exits and minimal foot traffic. Every detail mattered: she needed to control the environment without appearing conspicuous.

Using a burner phone, she sent a brief message, carefully worded: *"I have information regarding recent match selections that requires your attention. Meet me at the Corner Café, 5:30 p.m. No phones. Confidential."* She did not mention names, consequences, or sources. Curiosity, paired with his ambition, would compel him to respond.

As 5:30 approached, Avni positioned herself at a corner table, notebook and recorder-pen ready. She observed the entrance, noting anyone who lingered too long or glanced toward her. The street was calm, yet her instincts told her Singh's operatives could be watching.

A few minutes later, a tall, neatly dressed man entered, scanning the café before settling at a table nearby. His posture was confident, casual, but Avni recognized the telltale signs of caution in his eyes. Anil had the air of a man who believed himself in control, yet was aware that missteps could be costly.

Avni waited, letting him acclimate, observing habits: the way he ordered, the way he surveyed the room, the subtle fidgeting of a hand near his satchel. She needed him to feel in command before she made her move.

When the moment arrived, she spoke softly, leaning just enough to be private. "Mr. Deshmukh, I have information that directly concerns your recent match selections. It's critical that you see this, but discretion is essential."

The man's eyes narrowed, interest piqued, yet caution remained. Avni knew she had a narrow window to capture his attention, and cooperation.

Avni slid a small, inconspicuous packet across the table toward Anil. It contained a single email, carefully selected to demonstrate the network's reach without revealing everything at once. She watched his fingers hover over it, the subtle tightening of his jaw betraying a mix of curiosity and apprehension.

"This email," she said quietly, "shows directives for player substitutions, sent from Singh's account. You authorized some of these. I'm not here to accuse, just to offer a choice: cooperate, or risk being implicated if this surfaces."

Anil leaned back, eyes scanning the street outside as if expecting someone to appear. His fingers drummed against the table, a slow, deliberate rhythm. "And what do you want from me?" he asked, voice measured but cautious.

"Information," Avni replied. "Details only you can provide. Names, instructions, meeting minutes. Proof that can stand up independently. We take it step by step, safely, and build a case that exposes Singh without immediate danger to yourself."

The man paused, then exhaled slowly. "You've come prepared," he said, almost grudgingly. "Most people would try intimidation first. I see you understand the rules of this…game."

Avni inclined her head slightly. "I understand the stakes. One wrong move, and all of us could pay. But with careful steps, this can end differently, for you, for others, and for cricket itself."

Anil's gaze dropped to the packet, then back to her. "Alright," he whispered. "I'll cooperate. But you must guarantee anonymity at first. If Singh suspects, I'm finished."

Avni nodded, internally calculating contingencies for every possible leak. This was the breakthrough she had been seeking: another critical link willing to act. Singh's network, once impenetrable, was beginning to yield to strategy, patience, and the trail Vihaan had left behind.

The first ripple had been created. The tide against the syndicate was building.

CHAPTER : 8

THE NET TIGHTENS

Avni returned to the safe house with a renewed sense of momentum. Rakesh's digital logs and Anil's insider confirmations were no longer isolated shards, they were converging into a coherent architecture of influence. She set her laptop on the table, opened a fresh timeline file, and began synthesizing the streams of evidence: timestamps, wire transfers, meeting minutes, and the coded entries from Vihaan's notebook.

The map she built on screen looked less like a conspiracy theory and more like a prosecutable case. Dates aligned: payments flowed the night before suspicious substitutions; shell entities reappeared whenever a contested bid for a stadium contract was awarded; the same courier company showed up in photographs taken at charity galas and in ledger receipts tied to offshore accounts. Each node she connected tightened the noose around Singh's network.

Avni paused at a line linking a high- profile politician to a satellite company that had issued invoices for services never rendered. The invoices matched ledger entries in Raghav's folder; the payment trails reappeared in Rakesh's logs. The corruption was systemic, money routed through legitimate channels to mask illicit intent. She felt the sick thrill of clarity: exposure would reverberate beyond cricket, reaching into civic institutions that had long profited from willful blindness.

She compiled a prioritized action list. First: secure independent verification for three of the largest transfers, solid anchors that a court or a reputable publication could not easily dismiss. Second: arrange protected testimony for Rakesh and Anil, with recorded statements and corroborating logs. Third: prepare an editorial strategy, selective release, timed to minimize immediate risk to sources while maximizing public pressure.

Outside, Pune moved through its evening rituals: chai stalls closing, traffic thinning, a city unaware that its sports and civic image teetered on a single thread. Avni saved her work and sat back. The net was no longer theoretical. It was tangible, and it was beginning to tighten.

Avni leaned over the timeline, cross-referencing the new data from Anil with Rakesh's logs. Each entry became a building block in the syndicate's architecture: patterns of influence, payments, and match manipulations emerged like a living organism. Every official, every player, every shell company now had a name, a role, and a connection to Singh.

She paused at a photograph showing Singh at a mid-level board meeting, casually exchanging an envelope with a selector. The ledger from Rakesh confirmed the exact sum, and Vihaan's notes matched the unusual substitutions that followed that week. The precision of the syndicate's operations was breathtaking and terrifying.

Her next task was critical: establishing the chain of command. Singh was the nucleus, but the network depended on layers of subordinates who executed orders without question. If she could identify the intermediaries, she could disrupt the system gradually, reducing risk while building irrefutable evidence.

Avni began color-coding the chart: red for top-level operatives, orange for mid-level managers, and yellow for players and minor accomplices. By the time she finished, the map resembled a web of power radiating outward from Singh, each strand shimmering with potential exposure points.

The clock ticked past midnight. Avni, exhausted but alert, reviewed the compiled emails, meeting logs, and financial records once more. She annotated inconsistencies, highlighted patterns, and noted potential witnesses. Every step had to be deliberate, any premature move could alert Singh and compromise months of painstaking work.

Finally, she closed the laptop, leaning back and taking a deep breath. The net was real, the pieces aligned, and the first cracks in Singh's empire were no longer theoretical. Tomorrow, she would begin reaching out to the next layer of operatives, carefully choosing who could be trusted, who could be pressured, and who could deliver the evidence needed to bring the syndicate to its knees.

Avni began the morning by prioritizing targets: who could corroborate documentation without immediately endangering himself, and who might crack under pressure. She drafted a careful approach for each category. For mid- level operatives, accountants, match managers, and logistics coordinators, she planned a combination of small, verifiable requests and assurances of staged anonymity. For players and low- level staff, she prepared moral appeals and the promise of protection; for high- profile officials, she would need irrefutable paper trails before any public move.

Her first operational objective: secure three independent verifications of the largest transfers. Rakesh could provide logs; Anil could supply contextual minutes; Raghav's old receipts could bridge the gap to offshore routing. Those three anchors, corroborated independently, would transform suspicion into a case editors and prosecutors could not ignore.

She also developed an interrogative protocol, questions designed to elicit names, dates, and corroborating details without triggering panic. Each meeting would begin with soft prompts: "Tell me about the paperwork you handled that week," "What did the minutes say about player rotation?", leading to harder inquiries only when trust was established. Avni rehearsed scripts, anticipating evasions and rehearsing follow- ups that would close gaps without exposing sources.

Security planning ran parallel. She arranged rotating safe locations, staggered meeting times, and emergency signals with Rakesh and Anil. Burner phones remained the only line of contact; no emails with attachments until multiple confirmations existed offline. She prepared a contingency: if any source vanished or recanted, the evidence trail would still stand, cross- stamped receipts, independent timestamps, and cached bank logs.

By midday, the plan was drafted, the risks mapped, and the next calls scheduled. Avni felt the familiar tension, the mixture of exhaustion and exhilaration that accompanies the start of a pivotal operation. The net was tightening, but so was the necessity for precision. One misstep could cost lives; one carefully executed step could change the game forever.

Avni's first call went to a quiet number Rakesh had given her, a liaison at a small auditing firm who had previously processed some of the stadium's invoices. The woman on the line, Meera, was brusque but not unkind; she agreed to an in- person review provided anonymity and a plausible pretext. Avni felt a rush of relief. Meera's cooperation could supply an impartial confirmation of invoice irregularities, one of the independent anchors she needed.

Next she arranged to meet a logistics manager who'd handled equipment shipments for Singh's events. He was lower on the ladder but present at many gatherings; his testimony could connect envelopes and receipts to real movements. Avni scripted the meeting carefully: neutral language, sympathetic posture, and an offer of staggered disclosure to keep pressure manageable.

Security remained omnipresent in her plans. She instructed Rakesh to transfer selected logs only via physical USB drives left at dead- drop locations, no emails, no cloud links. Anil would prepare signed minutes with redacted identifiers that still demonstrated manipulation. Raghav agreed to contact one former courier who might corroborate deliveries. Each small corroboration, taken together, would form the scaffolding of a case that could survive scrutiny.

As evening approached, Avni felt the familiar ache, hunger tempered by adrenaline, but she pressed on, compiling, annotating, and encrypting backups. She created two parallel evidence stacks: one fragile, for controlled sharing with trusted journalists and lawyers; the other, an immutable archive stored offline in multiple secure locations.

Before bed, she left one final instruction with Rakesh: "If anything looks off, burn the backups and disappear for twenty- four hours." The note was grim but necessary. The hunt for truth had sharpened into a strategy of survival as well as exposure. Tomorrow she would meet Meera and the logistics manager; each conversation had to be precise, humane, and untraceable. The net tightened and Avni had to be the one to pull it closed.

The morning meeting with Meera was efficient and discreet. She arrived at a neutral co- working space, carrying a plain canvas bag and a guarded expression. Meera's demeanor was professional, precise answers, clipped sentences, but when Avni showed her a cropped invoice and a highlighted bank reference, the woman's facade slipped.

"These figures shouldn't exist," Meera murmured, tapping the screen. "They don't match procurement. Whoever authorized this routed payments through intermediary vendors that don't supply anything here." Her fingers danced across the keyboard as she walked Avni through the audit trail, vendor IDs that resolved to shell addresses, payment beneficiaries who dissolved after a few transactions, and routing numbers linked to offshore accounts. "You can't publish this without legal backing," she warned, "but this is authentic."

Relief and dread rose together in Avni. One anchor secured. One more verified thread stitched into the case. She thanked Meera, offering a plan for staggered disclosures and insisting on minimal electronic exchange. Meera agreed to produce a signed summary, on paper, if Avni could guarantee secure delivery.

The logistics manager meeting that afternoon produced a different kind of evidence. Quiet, weary, and clearly uncomfortable with memory, he described late- night pickups and courier codes, phrases used instead of names, numbered envelopes handed over in hotel corridors, and a recurring van with an unremarkable company logo. "We called it 'Package A'," he said. "Never asked what was inside." He produced a manifest, dates, pickup times, and vehicle numbers, that matched several photographs in Avni's folder.

As the day waned, however, an uneasy pattern emerged. At both meetings, a nondescript white car had been parked nearby, first at a distance, then closer. Someone was tracking her movements. The evidence stack had grown heavier; so had the shadow trailing it.

Avni left the evening with confirmation and new urgency: the syndicate's mechanics were now proven on paper and in testimony, but time was closing fast. She needed to secure the signed summaries and relocate the archives, immediately.

Avni returned to the safe house, alert to every shadow and reflective surface along Pune's narrow streets. The white car from earlier had vanished, but the unease lingered; Singh's operatives were patient and observant. She locked the door, checked the perimeter, and finally exhaled.

She laid out the signed summary from Meera and the courier manifests from the logistics manager, aligning them with Rakesh and Anil's contributions. Together, the documents formed a lattice of verification, each layer reinforcing the next. The trail was now undeniable: invoices, transfers, meeting logs, and firsthand accounts converged in a coherent narrative of corruption and manipulation.

Avni began digitizing the paper records, using an offline scanner connected to a secure laptop she had never connected to the internet. Each file was encrypted and backed up in multiple drives, all stored in separate hidden compartments. One copy went into a fireproof safe; another, disguised in everyday items, was set aside for emergency relocation.

Her mind shifted to strategy. Singh's network could not be toppled in a single strike; premature exposure could backfire, endangering her and her sources. Stepwise dismantling was essential, approach the mid-level operatives, secure their cooperation, and then link their testimonies to top-tier officials. With each verified thread, pressure on Singh would increase while minimizing immediate risk.

Avni also reviewed contingencies. If her safe house was compromised, she had secondary locations, backup drives, and disposable communication methods. She planned staggered meetings, randomized times, and alternated travel routes to minimize predictability. Every precaution was necessary; the stakes were escalating.

By nightfall, Avni felt a mix of exhaustion and grim determination. The net was real, tightening around Singh's empire. Every thread she had secured, every testimony verified, brought her closer to exposing the full scale of deception and closer to the inevitable confrontation with the syndicate itself.

The next morning, Avni convened a discreet meeting with Rakesh and Anil at a secluded part of Pune, far from familiar streets. They arrived separately, alert and cautious, each carrying documentation that had been meticulously prepared for offline transfer. Avni outlined the day's objectives: verify remaining questionable transactions, cross-check meeting minutes, and identify the next tier of operatives whose cooperation could expose Singh's upper network.

Rakesh presented additional bank logs, encrypted and time-stamped, showing repeated transfers routed through shell entities. Each transaction correlated to a match where unexpected player substitutions had occurred. Avni carefully noted the patterns and compared them with Vihaan's notebook entries; the synchronicity left no room for doubt.

Anil provided copies of sensitive meeting minutes with coded directives for player rotations and team selection, partially redacted to protect his identity. These minutes, when juxtaposed with the financial records, revealed how Singh's instructions were operationalized across multiple levels of management and selection. Every directive aligned perfectly with manipulated match outcomes, building an undeniable chain from the top of the syndicate down to individual actions.

Avni mapped the connections visually on a large board, linking names, dates, and financial trails. Lines radiated outward from Singh to officials, selectors, and players, forming a network that was both complex and fragile. The three of them reviewed the map, identifying nodes that could be pressured for corroboration and gaps that still required verification.

Security remained paramount. Avni assigned staggered movement schedules for each participant and arranged secure drop locations for all sensitive materials. Burner phones were the only line of communication, and any digital traces were strictly avoided.

By the end of the day, the team had successfully verified multiple evidence points and identified the next layer of key players for engagement. The net around Singh's empire was constricting, and Avni knew each step forward was as dangerous as it was necessary.

Avni spent the early evening preparing for her first direct engagement with a mid-level operative: Sunil Patil, a logistics coordinator responsible for event planning and equipment transport. Unlike Rakesh or Anil, Sunil had access to operational details but no formal authority. His testimony could directly link shipments, envelopes, and financial transfers to Singh's directives, forming another critical bridge in the case.

She reviewed every piece of evidence he could corroborate: manifests, photographs, and internal memos. Her approach had to be subtle, too much pressure would make him panic, too little would produce vague, noncommittal responses. Avni rehearsed questions designed to encourage recall without fear: "Walk me through last month's delivery schedules," "Who authorized changes to shipment times?" Each inquiry would be a stepping stone to uncovering more about the syndicate's methods.

Security measures were equally meticulous. The meeting location was a small, inconspicuous café in Pune, chosen for multiple exits and a clear view of the street. Burner phones were used to coordinate arrival times, and Avni preprogrammed contingencies: safe routes, escape plans, and drop-off points for any sensitive materials Sunil might provide.

As the hour approached, Avni reviewed the dossier one last time. She had arranged for discreet recording equipment hidden in a pen, a set of offline copies of key documents, and preprinted forms to obtain signed acknowledgments. She also briefed Rakesh and Anil on staggered check-ins, ensuring someone would notice if she failed to return on schedule.

The first step in engaging Sunil would test both her strategic planning and her ability to navigate human psychology under pressure. This meeting could either unlock a wealth of operational insight or raise the first red flag to Singh's network. Avni took a deep breath, mentally preparing herself. Tonight, the net would tighten further.

Sunil arrived cautiously, scanning the café before taking a seat across from Avni. He was wiry, mid-thirties, and clearly nervous, his hands trembled slightly as he set down a leather folder. Avni smiled reassuringly, keeping her tone calm and neutral. "Thank you for coming," she began. "I just need you to walk me through your role in the last few events. Nothing more. Just facts."

Sunil exhaled, the tension in his shoulders easing slightly. He opened the folder, revealing detailed delivery manifests, handwritten notes, and copies of internal memos. Avni leaned in subtly, letting him guide the conversation. “Tell me about the shipments that occurred the week before the Pune charity match,” she prompted.

He spoke in quiet, deliberate tones. “Packages labeled A, B, and C. Envelope deliveries at odd hours. Instructions always came via encrypted emails, then confirmed in person with a sealed stamp. I never questioned who authorized them, I just followed protocol.”

Avni cross-referenced each detail with photographs, ledgers, and bank transfers. Every number, date, and signature matched the evidence she already held. Her eyes flicked to the pen recorder, hidden in her hand, capturing every word.

“You’re doing the right thing by telling the truth,” Avni said softly. “If you cooperate, it’s controlled. You’ll provide the details, and we can ensure protection and anonymity while the bigger picture comes together.”

Sunil nodded slowly, beginning to feel the gravity of the choice in front of him. His testimony could now link envelopes, shipments, and accounts directly to Singh’s operational commands. For the first time, he realized he could be part of dismantling the network, or if mishandled, become collateral damage.

By the end of the meeting, Avni had documented precise details from Sunil that could bridge the operational and financial evidence. Another crucial piece of the puzzle was secured, and the net around Singh’s empire tightened further.

Back at the safe house, Avni carefully organized Sunil's testimony alongside Rakesh and Anil's contributions. Each set of documents, emails, and witness statements now formed a cohesive network: operational actions linked to financial flows, directives connected to outcomes, and key individuals mapped within Singh's hierarchy. The net, once abstract, was now a tangible framework ready to be used strategically.

Avni began creating a prioritized action plan. Sunil's detailed account of deliveries and envelopes could directly implicate mid-level operatives and provide corroboration for bank transfers. The next phase would be to approach additional insiders who held unique access to records or communications, always ensuring staggered contact and maximum security.

She color-coded the evidence, connecting names, dates, and events across different mediums. Red lines indicated confirmed actions with signatures and timestamps; orange lines represented unverified but highly likely connections; yellow lines marked potential leads requiring further validation. By the end of the mapping session, Singh's empire looked both sprawling and vulnerable.

Security remained paramount. Avni stored physical documents in separate hidden compartments, duplicated drives in secure locations, and encrypted digital copies offline. Burner phones were scheduled for intermittent checks, ensuring no predictable patterns for surveillance. Every precaution was designed to protect her, her sources, and the integrity of the evidence.

As night fell over Pune, Avni reviewed the consolidated network once more. The gaps were narrowing; the links were undeniable. Singh's once-impenetrable operations now had vulnerabilities, each layer exposed by careful planning, corroborated testimony, and meticulous analysis.

The next steps would require courage, discretion, and calculated pressure. The net was ready to constrict. Singh's control over the cricketing world was weakening, and Avni knew that each move forward could bring her closer to truth and to danger.

CHAPTER : 9

BREAKING THE SILENCE

Avni stared at the evidence map pinned across the safe house wall, the colored threads converging on one name: Vikram Singh. The empire he had built, of bribes, threats, and silent obedience, was no longer just rumor or suspicion. She now possessed irrefutable proof. But evidence alone meant nothing unless it reached the right hands and the right audience. It was time to plan exposure.

Her first step was controlled dissemination. She couldn't release everything at once; the syndicate would bury or discredit it before it gained traction. Instead, she would leak fragments, small, undeniable truths that forced public attention, while keeping the larger archive hidden until the world was watching.

Avni drafted a blueprint for her exposure strategy. The opening move would be to share redacted excerpts of Sunil's testimony with a trusted senior journalist at a national daily, someone too visible to silence quickly, yet cautious enough to protect the source. Parallel to this, she would feed corroborating data to an independent sports watchdog, ensuring that multiple voices amplified the same story.

She also contacted a discreet legal advisor, outlining her intent to publish without revealing her identity as the primary investigator. The lawyer agreed to create legal buffers: anonymous submissions, whistleblower clauses, and contingency measures in case the syndicate struck back through courts or intimidation.

All the while, Avni kept her sources at the center of her plan. Rakesh, Anil, and Sunil had entrusted her with their truth, and protecting them was non-negotiable. She arranged safe contact points, relocation options, and even drafted escape strategies should Singh's men trace their involvement.

As she finalized the first leak package, documents anonymized, dates blurred but still credible, Avni felt the weight of the moment. The silence that had shielded Singh for decades was about to fracture. The first crack was ready.

The following morning, Avni arrived at a bustling Pune café, chosen for its anonymity among the crowds. She carried only a slim folder with carefully redacted excerpts, snippets of Sunil's testimony, paired with cross-checked invoices and shipment manifests. Across from her sat Kavita Deshmukh, a senior investigative journalist with decades of experience and a reputation for courage.

Avni slid the folder across the table, her voice low. "I need you to see this. But understand, it's only the surface."

Kavita adjusted her glasses and began scanning the pages. Her expression, usually unreadable, shifted subtly with each line. She paused at the memo bearing Singh's coded directives. "This isn't rumor," she whispered. "These are verifiable records."

Avni nodded. "There's more. But it has to be staged. If you print too much too soon, Singh's network will shut it down, discredit you, or worse. I need you to release this carefully, strategically."

Kavita tapped the folder, her journalistic instincts already at work. "A controlled leak, then. Enough to draw attention, but not enough for them to destroy the trail." She leaned in, her tone soft but resolute. "You're risking everything."

"So are you," Avni replied.

That evening, Kavita's article went live online: a crisp, surgical piece hinting at corruption within Pune's cricketing administration. It referenced "unnamed insiders," highlighted suspicious financial irregularities, and hinted at links to larger syndicates. It didn't name Singh outright, but anyone who understood the sport's power structure could see the shadow it cast.

Within hours, the story trended on social media. Commentators debated, fans speculated, and former players demanded answers. The cricket board issued a dismissive statement, calling it "baseless speculation." But Avni recognized the tremor beneath their denial, the silence around Singh had cracked.

The ripple had begun.

By midnight, Avni's burner phone buzzed relentlessly with updates. Social feeds pulsed with outrage: fans demanded accountability, hashtags spread like wildfire, and former cricketers split into camps, some dismissing the article, others admitting the allegations echoed whispers they'd heard for years.

Avni watched from the dimly lit safe house, every flicker of the screen reflecting both triumph and danger. Singh's name was not printed, yet his lieutenants recognized the implications immediately. She expected them to respond, and they did, swiftly.

The cricket board held a press conference the next morning, denouncing the report as "irresponsible journalism." They framed it as a smear campaign against the sport itself, urging fans to "respect the sanctity of cricket." The statement reeked of defensive posturing, but to the untrained eye, it sounded authoritative.

Avni took notes, dissecting every phrase. Their response was too aggressive for a baseless claim; it confirmed they felt the heat. Then came the countermove: Kavita's newsroom received veiled threats, phone calls warning her to "drop the story," anonymous emails filled with vague but menacing language. She called Avni in the late evening.

"They know I have more," Kavita said, her voice steady but tired. "They're testing how far I'll go."

Avni's grip tightened on the phone. "Hold your ground, but don't overplay it yet. I'll feed you the next piece soon. Smaller, sharper. Enough to keep them off balance."

Even as she spoke, Avni noticed something outside the window, a car idling too long, headlights dimmed. She closed the curtains quickly, her pulse racing. Singh's men were closing in, not just in the media but in the shadows of Pune's streets.

The backlash was real. The counterstrike had begun.

The next morning, Avni awoke to the sound of rain tapping against the shutters, the gray Pune skyline cloaked in monsoon mist. She checked her perimeter first, windows secured, cameras in place, backup drives hidden in their compartments. The white sedan she had spotted the night before was gone, but unease lingered like a shadow in the room. Singh's network was watching; she could feel it.

She spread the evidence across her desk once more, layering Sunil's testimony with Meera's audit trail and Anil's coded meeting minutes. The first leak had stirred the waters; now the second had to pierce deeper. She selected a packet of documents exposing irregular cash transfers tied to *youth cricket programs*. Framing the next leak around the exploitation of young players, rather than finances alone, would strike a nerve with the public. It would humanize the corruption.

Her plan was simple but sharp: release the second wave through an independent sports watchdog based outside

India. The syndicate could intimidate local journalists, but international attention would force transparency. Avni prepared the files carefully, redacted names, blurred account numbers, but enough hard detail to prove authenticity.

She encrypted the documents and passed them to Rakesh, instructing him to use a one-time secure relay from an overseas server. "No repeats, no trace. This has to vanish after it's sent," she reminded him. He nodded grimly.

Meanwhile, Avni adjusted her own routine: shorter trips, randomized routes, and staged appearances in public spaces to mask her movements. She knew Singh's watchers would attempt to corner her soon. Every leak tightened the noose, not just around Singh's empire, but also around her own freedom.

Tonight, the second crack would open. And the storm was only beginning.

Two days later, the international watchdog published Avni's second leak under the headline: *"Youth Cricket Programs Exploited: Millions Diverted Through Shadow Accounts."* The report detailed how money intended for training camps, equipment, and scholarships had been siphoned into shell companies, while young players were left with crumbling facilities and broken promises.

The story hit harder than Avni anticipated. Parents of aspiring cricketers flooded social media with anger. Former juniors came forward, sharing their own experiences of abandoned trials, withheld payments, and inexplicable rejections despite stellar performance. The watchdog's global credibility shielded the report from easy dismissal, and for the first time, international news outlets picked up the story. Headlines from London to Sydney echoed the same sentiment: *India's beloved game was being betrayed from within.*

The cricket board scrambled. They announced an "internal inquiry," but their statement lacked conviction. Sponsors began issuing cautious remarks, some even threatening to withdraw funding if the allegations proved true. Avni saw the shift immediately, money, the syndicate's lifeblood, was under scrutiny.

That night, Kavita called again. "Your timing was perfect," she said. "The board's panicking. But they'll come after us harder now. I've already noticed plainclothes men loitering outside the newsroom."

Avni tightened her jaw. "Keep the focus on the story. I'll handle the shadows."

After the call, she checked her hidden drives once more, then glanced out of the window. The same white sedan was back, parked across the street, its windshield glistening in the rain. This time, Avni didn't close the curtains. She stared directly at the car, letting whoever sat inside know she had seen them.

The silence outside was heavy. The world was finally listening, but Singh's men were no longer content to watch from afar.

By dawn, the pressure had escalated. Avni awoke to find a plain envelope slipped under the safe house door. No markings, no return address, just a single sheet of paper inside. The message was typed in bold, deliberate words:

"Stop, or you'll end up like him."

Beneath the line was a faded photograph, Coach Ashok Tilekar, smiling in an old team picture. The implication was chilling, and Avni's grip on the page tightened until her knuckles turned white. Singh's men were no longer just circling; they were warning her that she was next.

She forced herself to breathe evenly, methodically placing the envelope in a sealed evidence bag. Fear was a weapon Singh wielded as effectively as money, and she could not allow it to derail her. But the message had sharpened the stakes, her timeline for exposure was narrowing.

That afternoon, while moving through a crowded Pune market, Avni noticed a man following her at a distance. He pretended to browse stalls whenever she turned, his reflection catching briefly in shop windows. She altered her route twice, and he adjusted each time. Singh's watchers were testing her nerve in public now.

Avni ducked into a side alley, heart pounding, and waited until the man passed. When he was gone, she pulled out her burner phone and sent a single coded text to Rakesh: *"The storm is here."* Within minutes, he confirmed new safe transport routes and a fallback location should the safe house be compromised.

Back inside, Avni began preparing the third wave of leaks, this time more explosive, implicating specific board officials by name. If Singh wanted to play intimidation, she would respond with precision strikes. Every threat only pushed her closer to revealing the full truth.

The confrontation was no longer distant. It was unfolding in real time.

Avni moved with the cold, focused urgency of someone who's come to accept that reckless courage must be married to calculation. The third leak would name board officials, men whose signatures appeared beside the largest transfers and whose voices had shielded Singh in public. She drafted the dossier carefully: direct invoices, matching meeting minutes, photograph timestamps, and voice-matched snippets from the pen recorder. Each allegation was paired with at least two independent confirmations to blunt any attempt at discreditation.

She coordinated with Kavita and the legal adviser. The lawyer insisted on last-minute redactions for safety, protective anonymization for lower-level witnesses and legal phrasing that left no room for libel suits. Kavita arranged the editorial window: the piece would go live at 10:00 a.m., giving Avni time to move sources and create a public narrative that would be hard for the board to smother.

Avni checked on Rakesh, Anil, and Sunil one by one. They had been moved in stages, short relocations to throw off tailing, each placed with discreet hosts until the leak landed. She left contingency funds, burner phones, and instructions: if anyone felt at immediate risk, they were to vanish for forty-eight hours and wait for a prearranged signal. The weight of responsibility pressed on her, these were not abstract sources; they were people whose lives could unravel.

To blunt predictable surveillance, Avni arranged a diversion: Raghav would stage a call to a local sports club hinting at a rival exposé, drawing Singh's watchers toward a false lead. It was a small, risky theatre of deception, but she needed Singh's eyes distracted when the truth hit.

At 9:30 a.m., Avni uploaded the final, encrypted package to the watchdog and sent the go-ahead text to Kavita. Her hands trembled only once, briefly, before she steadied them. The dossier was out of her safe hands and into the waiting world, and with it, the slow, dangerous machinery of consequence began to turn. The clock ticked toward ten.

At ten on the dot, Kavita's byline lit up on the homepage. The dossier dropped like a bomb, photographs, invoices, meeting minutes, and the redacted names of officials tied directly to Singh's accounts. The article named men previously untouchable and laid out the financial logic in clinical, undeniable terms. For a moment the newsroom hummed like an engine firing on all cylinders; outside, Pune's feeds exploded.

Within an hour, the reaction was seismic. Opposition politicians called for a parliamentary probe. Sponsors froze payments and released statements expressing "grave concern." Former players, some long silent, posted testimonies that, once unshackled, multiplied like embers catching a wind. The hashtag #CricketNotCorruption trended across platforms, and editors elsewhere began to pick up the thread. The silence Avni had broken now echoed around the world.

But victory and peril arrived together. Singh's PR machine moved instantly, producing a polished denial and an accusation of fabricated evidence. His lieutenants launched coordinated disinformation: anonymous posts questioning Kavita's sources, edits of old footage showing official events, and thinly veiled threats aimed at journalists. Within hours, a legal notice arrived at Kavita's office alleging "defamation and malicious intent." The board called for calm and announced a panel to "review governance processes."

At the safe house, Avni watched the feeds with a detached, fierce attention. The public pressure was working, but the danger curve had steepened. Rakesh and Anil had been successful in creating corroboration; Sunil's operational confirmations had made the narrative airtight. Yet she could already sense Singh's next move: discredit the sources, intimidate the witnesses, and bury the story in litigation and counterclaims.

A knock sounded at the safe house door that evening, soft, methodical. Avni froze, the taste of iron in her mouth. She peered through the peephole and saw a familiar figure: Inspector Jamkar. His expression was unreadable, the rain dampening his coat. He spoke low through the door: “We need to talk. Now.”

Avni’s pulse quickened. Jamkar had always walked a fine line between ally and adversary, but his arrival now, unannounced, on the heels of the dossier’s release, was unsettling. She unlatched the door cautiously, keeping the chain hooked. His eyes met hers, steady, shadowed with something she couldn’t name.

“You shouldn’t be here,” she said quietly.

“I shouldn’t be anywhere,” he replied, his tone flat. “They’ve put a price on my head too. May I come in?”

Rakesh rose from the sofa, a hand brushing the edge of the cricket bat propped near the wall as though instinctively reaching for a weapon. Kavita looked up from her laptop, her face taut with worry. Sunil, still cross-checking statements, narrowed his eyes. After a pause heavy enough to crush breath, Avni slid the chain free.

Jamkar entered, dripping water onto the floorboards. He scanned the room, then lowered his voice. “Singh’s men are moving faster than you think. Half the syndicate believes I fed you information. They’re planning to erase the trail, witnesses, documents, and anyone linked to this story.” His gaze shifted deliberately to Kavita.

“What do you want from us?” Avni asked.

“To survive,” Jamkar said simply. “And to finally put Singh in a cage. But you don’t have much time. They’ll come for this place tonight.”

The group exchanged uneasy looks. The safe house, which had felt like their last bastion of secrecy, suddenly seemed porous, fragile. Rakesh swore under his breath.

“Why should we trust you?” Sunil challenged.

Jamkar’s lips curved into a grim half-smile. He reached into his coat and placed a small recorder on the table. “Because I’ve been recording every meeting with Singh for the last three years. And because if you fall, I fall too.”

The room went utterly silent. Outside, thunder rolled across Pune’s skies.

Avni stared at the recorder as though it were a loaded gun. Its presence changed the entire equation. If Jamkar was telling the truth, this was not just corroboration, it was dynamite. Years of covert conversations, threats, promises, and deals could be contained within that small device.

Kavita leaned forward, her journalist’s instincts ignited. “If this is real, it can collapse Singh’s empire overnight,” she whispered, fingers trembling slightly.

Jamkar nodded. “But only if used correctly. Singh has layers of protection, political, financial, and physical. If you dump everything at once, it might vanish in legal quicksand. You need precision. Strike at the one point he can't protect."

Rakesh exhaled sharply, pacing the narrow room. "You mean the cricket board elections," he muttered, as though piecing together a puzzle. "He's installing his man as president next month. If the evidence lands just before that, it'll fracture his control."

Sunil, skeptical yet compelled, folded his arms. "And you're offering this… why? Because you want him out, or because you're already compromised?"

Jamkar's jaw tightened. "Both. I've played both sides too long. I thought I could contain the damage, steer him away from bloodier choices. But the coach's death…" His voice faltered, just enough to betray a crack. "That was my breaking point."

Avni's mind raced. Trusting Jamkar could be the turning point, or the trap that destroyed them all. She looked at her allies: Kavita, alight with conviction; Rakesh, bristling with protective anger; Sunil, guarded yet calculating.

Finally, she met Jamkar's eyes. "Then you stay here tonight," she said. "If Singh's men are coming, we'll face them together."

The words hung in the dim room like an oath. Somewhere beyond, a car engine idled too long outside.

CHAPTER : 10

- - - - - - - - - - - -

THE SIEGE BEGINS

The night settled over Pune like a thick, suffocating blanket. Rain slicked streets reflected flickering streetlights as Avni reinforced every entry point in the safe house. Doors bolted, windows shuttered, and backup drives dispersed into hidden compartments. The air was tense, charged with anticipation, each creak of the floorboards magnified in the silence.

Jamkar sat across from her at the small dining table, his recorder still between them, now a symbol of both leverage and danger. Kavita typed feverishly on her laptop, drafting articles that would be published only once the immediate threat passed. Rakesh checked the burner phones, repeating the emergency contact routine for the group, while Sunil meticulously reviewed witness statements and supporting evidence, preparing them for potential extraction.

Outside, headlights cut through the rain. Shadows of cars paused, idling just beyond the perimeter, scanning for movement. Avni's pulse quickened, but her mind remained razor-sharp. Singh's men were probing, testing defenses, waiting for a sign of weakness. Every second counted.

Avni pulled Jamkar aside. "Do you know how many are out there?" she asked quietly.

"Enough to take this house in under ten minutes if they coordinate," he replied grimly. "But they're waiting, seeing if we panic. That's their leverage."

She nodded. Calm was essential. She moved through the room, checking everyone's positioning and readiness. Phones, documents, and backup drives were strategically placed. Escape routes were mapped, signals rehearsed, and safe points designated.

As the first drops of rain splashed against the shuttered windows, a low hum of engines reached her ears—too synchronized to be casual. Avni's heart steadied. The siege had begun.

Outside, the shadowy figures were closing in. Inside, Avni and her allies prepared for the fight of their lives. The night would determine whether the truth survived or whether Singh's empire would strike back, unchallenged.

The hum of engines intensified, blending with the relentless patter of rain against the roof. Avni crouched by the window, peering through a narrow slit in the shutters. She could make out at least three vehicles, their headlights dimmed, circling the block in synchronized patterns. Singh's men were professionals; this wasn't a casual intimidation, it was a calculated test, a probe to gauge defenses and patience.

She turned to Jamkar. "Can we buy time?"

He nodded. “As long as we stay unpredictable. They’ll hesitate if they can’t locate our exact position. Keep calm, don’t engage unless they force it.”

Rakesh checked the burner phones again, confirming the safety lines. “If this escalates, we’ll signal for extraction. Everyone knows the plan,” he reminded the group, tension sharp in his voice.

Kavita saved a draft of the third leak, encrypted and ready to go. The timing had to be perfect. Too early, and Singh’s men could destroy evidence or intimidate sources; too late, and the opportunity to create public pressure would vanish.

Sunil, normally quiet, spoke up. “We need to consider contingencies if they breach the perimeter. Routes, signals, fallback points, all of it.”

Avni outlined the exit strategy: staggered egress points, separate transport for evidence, and preplanned rendezvous locations across Pune. She emphasized discipline, no panic, no deviations, and no solo moves.

Then, without warning, a black SUV slowed near the front gate. Its engine idled low, doors locked, the driver’s face obscured by shadows. Avni held her breath. The siege had escalated from observation to direct confrontation. Every second now was a test of nerves, preparation, and the team’s cohesion.

Inside the safe house, the small group exchanged determined glances. They knew one thing with absolute clarity: the night would not end quietly.

The black SUV crept closer, stopping just outside the gate. Avni crouched low, signaling the group to remain silent. Rain dripped steadily from the eaves, masking the subtle hum of approaching vehicles. Two more cars had joined the perimeter, completing a near-complete blockade. Singh's men were precise, professionals who had mapped the neighborhood in advance.

Jamkar whispered, "They're testing our reactions. If we flinch, they move in." He gestured toward the rear exit. "That's our contingency if they make a first strike."

Avni positioned herself near the reinforced door, eyes flicking between the street and the interior of the safe house. Rakesh held a small, metal rod for defense, while Sunil clutched the manifest copies, the most vulnerable evidence. Kavita sat behind a reinforced table, laptop ready to transmit the third leak at a moment's notice.

Suddenly, a figure emerged from the shadows, moving deliberately toward the front gate. Avni recognized the uniform immediately, plain clothes, but the gait, the precision, unmistakable. She froze, counting heartbeats in silence, calculating distances.

"Don't engage yet," Jamkar hissed. "Wait for the signal. Let them think we're cornered."

The figure paused, scanning the area, then circled toward the rear as if testing the escape route. Avni exhaled slowly, motioning everyone to maintain their positions. The tension was unbearable; each second stretched like hours.

Then, a low whistle cut through the rain, a prearranged signal from Singh's second-in-command. It was subtle, almost imperceptible, but Avni caught it immediately. The siege had escalated from observation to tactical probing.

Inside, the team braced themselves. Every plan, every precaution, was about to be tested under live fire. Tonight, the safe house was no longer a sanctuary, it was a battleground.

The quiet tension shattered as the first of Singh's operatives moved decisively. A loud metallic clank echoed from the front gate, the unmistakable sound of a crowbar levering at the lock. Avni signaled the team to take defensive positions, their nerves taut like drawn wires.

Jamkar whispered precise instructions. "Rakesh and I hold the front. Sunil, move the evidence to the secondary cache under the floorboards. Kavita, be ready to transmit the leak if this escalates." Each word was deliberate, a lifeline in the chaos.

The front gate groaned under repeated pressure, splintering slightly with each strike. Rain splashed into the narrow gaps, but inside, the team's focus sharpened.

Avni gripped a heavy metal rod, listening to the rhythm of the attackers' movements. Timing and anticipation were everything, one misstep could be fatal.

From the rear, the shadowy figure Jamkar had spotted circled closer. The backup route had been compromised faster than expected. Avni cursed under her breath; Singh had anticipated her contingencies.

A flash of movement caught her eye, the crowbar swung again, catching a fragment of light. The attackers were coordinated, moving like a single organism. Avni steadied her breathing, counting heartbeats, ready to strike only if forced.

Then Jamkar made the first move, stepping out from cover with calculated force, blocking the front approach while Rakesh flanked to intercept. The first operative hesitated, surprised by the sudden resistance. Avni seized the moment, driving the metal rod into the gap, forcing the attacker back.

The clash had begun in earnest. The safe house, once a bastion of secrecy, had become the epicenter of a deadly confrontation. Every second counted, and every action could tip the balance between survival and catastrophe.

The front gate shuddered with repeated blows as Singh's operatives tried to force entry. Rainwater poured through the gaps, soaking the floorboards, but the team inside remained laser-focused. Adrenaline sharpened senses; every creak and shadow became a potential threat.

Jamkar took the lead, blocking the front while Rakesh moved to flank, forcing the intruders into the narrow corridor. Avni stayed behind the table, gripping the metal rod, eyes scanning for any secondary breach points. Sunil worked frantically, sliding the evidence into hidden compartments beneath the floorboards, while Kavita readied her laptop to transmit the third leak if the attackers broke in.

The attackers' coordination was precise; they had clearly studied the safe house. Two more men appeared at the side entrance, attempting to overpower the locks. Avni's mind raced, there was no room for error. She pivoted, striking one with controlled force, buying critical seconds.

A crash echoed from the front gate, the crowbar had finally splintered the outer wood. One intruder's arm reached through the widening gap. Jamkar lunged, spinning the man back into the rain-soaked street. Rakesh intercepted another, throwing him off balance with a single, forceful shove. The chaos outside was mirrored by controlled precision inside.

Kavita's hands trembled as she typed, uploading encrypted packets of the third leak. Every keystroke mattered; one interruption could destroy the last remaining proof.

Avni glanced at Jamkar, a silent acknowledgment passing between them, they could hold for now, but the siege was far from over. Singh's men would regroup, and the night was far from finished. Every second of this struggle was critical: protect the evidence, protect the team, survive.

The battle had only just begun, and the stakes had never been higher.

Avni crouched behind the reinforced table, surveying the safe house with a strategic eye. The first wave of attackers had been repelled, but Singh's operatives were professional, they would return stronger, more coordinated. Every second they hesitated, she gained a precious window to consolidate defenses and secure the evidence.

Jamkar whispered across the room, "We need to anticipate their next move. They'll try the roof or the rear; they know the front is compromised."

Avni nodded, already calculating. She instructed Rakesh to barricade the rear doors with reinforced furniture and tie-down cables scavenged from storage. Sunil was ordered to relocate the remaining evidence into the hidden cavity beneath the false floorboards, ensuring it could not be seized even if the house were breached.

Kavita's laptop remained open, uploading the third leak in fragments. Avni monitored the progress, timing the packets to minimize risk of interception. Even a partial upload would suffice to trigger public scrutiny and force Singh's hand.

A muffled shout outside confirmed her suspicions, Singh's team was regrouping. She activated the safe house's security alarms, knowing the shrill warning could buy crucial seconds, sowing confusion among the attackers.

"Rakesh, block the rear stairwell. Jamkar, cover the front. Sunil, finish the evidence transfer. Kavita, stay ready," she commanded, her tone calm but urgent.

Outside, boots splashed through puddles, shadows moving with intent. Avni's team braced themselves, hearts synchronized to the rhythm of the storm. Every move they made was deliberate, precise, a ballet of survival.

The night had transformed from siege into calculated warfare. Singh's operatives had underestimated the resolve and preparation of their targets. Avni knew the evidence had to survive above all else; protecting it was the difference between exposing Singh and losing everything.

The next move would define the battle.

Rain hammered the safe house as Singh's operatives made their next move. This time, it was coordinated and aggressive: two men approached the rear stairwell while others circled toward the rooftop. The storm masked their approach, giving them the advantage of surprise.

Avni remained calm, every movement calculated. "Rakesh, intercept the rear. Jamkar, front. Sunil, secure the evidence now. Kavita, stay on the line," she ordered.

Rakesh waited in the shadows near the rear stairwell. As the first operative appeared, he lunged, using the element of surprise to shove the intruder off balance. The man recovered quickly, drawing a baton, but Rakesh blocked it, forcing him down the stairs. Avni joined, striking decisively to prevent pursuit.

On the front, Jamkar engaged another operative attempting to force the broken gate. His precision and strength were enough to push the man back into the rain. Avni's mind raced, this was not just about defending walls; it was about timing, misdirection, and protecting the evidence above all.

Meanwhile, Kavita's laptop pinged repeatedly. The upload of the third leak was progressing in fragmented bursts, carefully timed to avoid interception. Each successful transfer strengthened their leverage, ensuring Singh's men couldn't silence the story without facing immediate consequences.

The rooftop threat forced Avni's attention. She grabbed a heavy pipe and approached cautiously, forcing the intruder to retreat with a series of controlled strikes. His accomplice on the rear stairs stumbled, and Avni pressed the advantage, moving to barricade the stairwell with reinforced furniture.

By the end of the confrontation, Singh's operatives had been temporarily repelled, but the battle was far from over. Avni knew the siege would escalate, and every tactical decision from this point onward could be the difference between survival and disaster.

Avni studied the safe house's layout, heart steady despite the chaos outside. Singh's operatives were well-trained but predictable in their coordination. If she could exploit small fractures, miscommunication, impatience, fear, she could turn their aggression against them.

She whispered her plan to Jamkar and Rakesh. "Create controlled distractions. Make them believe they're surrounded on multiple fronts. Force them to split or hesitate. We can't overpower them head-on, but we can manipulate their moves."

Rakesh nodded, already sliding doors and furniture into makeshift barricades. Jamkar positioned himself to simulate movement across the front while Avni moved silently to the side corridor, prepared to trigger subtle noises, dropping a metal rod here, rattling a shutter there, to give the illusion of additional defenders.

Sunil, watching the rain-slicked street, was instructed to shine a flashlight intermittently across the perimeter, creating phantom shadows. Each signal had to appear uncoordinated, random, yet threatening enough to confuse the attackers.

Minutes passed like hours as Singh's men began reacting. Shouts echoed from the streets, footsteps scattered, and for the first time, a discordant rhythm emerged among them. Avni pressed the advantage, guiding Rakesh and Jamkar to intercept small groups, isolating them without exposing the main entrances.

Inside, Kavita monitored the upload, ensuring the third leak continued without interruption. The evidence, now partially public, served as both shield and leverage. Every second that Singh's operatives hesitated increased the chance of survival for the team and the documents.

By late night, a tactical stalemate had formed. Singh's men were frustrated, cautious, and beginning to suspect traps at every turn. Avni allowed herself a brief, calculated breath, her counter-strategy had worked. The safe house held, and the night was still theirs.

The quiet lull was deceptive. Avni sensed it immediately, the tension outside had thickened, the footsteps and whispers replaced by heavy engines and low, coordinated voices. Reinforcements. Singh had called in heavier backup, men trained to storm, intimidate, and eliminate resistance. The siege was escalating.

Inside the safe house, Avni gathered the team. "They've brought the next wave," she said calmly, though her pulse thumped like a drum. "We need to hold, but also prepare for a tactical withdrawal if necessary. Evidence comes first, survival second, but both must happen."

Jamkar checked the firearms he had hidden under tables, weapons discreet but ready. "We can hold the main floors, but the rooftop and back are vulnerable. If they breach those, we move to the inner chamber and lock it down."

Rakesh and Sunil reinforced barricades at the rear and side exits. Every loose board, every furniture edge was strategically positioned to delay or injure the intruders, not just block them.

Avni reviewed the partial upload of the third leak. Every successful packet meant Singh's network would face global scrutiny within hours. That knowledge fueled her resolve. They were fighting not just for survival, but for truth, and every second bought time for exposure.

Outside, the engines roared closer, lights cutting through the sheets of rain. Figures appeared at the periphery, moving with lethal intent. Avni positioned herself near the central doorway, watching, listening, anticipating. The team synchronized movements, no one acted without a signal.

Tonight, the siege would peak. Singh's operatives were no longer probing, they were striking with intent. Avni's team had to repel the assault while safeguarding the evidence, knowing that one misstep could cost everything.

The storm outside mirrored the chaos inside, and the final confrontation had begun.

The first strike hit like a thunderclap. A battering ram crashed against the front barricade, splintering wood and sending shards across the floor. Singh's operatives were inside now, their movements swift, calculated, and merciless. Avni braced herself, signaling the team to hold positions.

Jamkar engaged the nearest intruder, grappling and forcing him toward the front door where Rakesh struck with precision, buying crucial seconds. Sunil slid the remaining evidence under the reinforced floor panel, securing it in a cavity only he and Avni knew. Kavita clutched her laptop, ready to transmit the final fragments of the third leak at a moment's notice.

Rainwater dripped through the shattered windows, soaking the floor and making every movement treacherous. Adrenaline sharpened Avni's focus; every step, every swing of the rod was deliberate, aimed to control space, delay the attackers, and protect the team.

One operative lunged from the shadows, but Avni anticipated the strike, parrying and pushing him back toward a barricade. The confined space worked in their favor; the attackers' coordination faltered as each encounter became a separate skirmish.

The clash was relentless. Yells, splintering wood, and the metallic clang of improvised defenses filled the safe house. Yet amidst the chaos, Avni's mind remained sharp. She tracked every movement, calculated every response, and ensured the evidence, decades of corruption, witness statements, financial records, remained untouched.

Minutes stretched into what felt like hours, but slowly, the tide shifted. Singh's men, frustrated and disoriented, began to retreat toward the streets, regrouping to plan their next assault. Avni exhaled, exhaustion pressing into her muscles, yet a fierce resolve remained.

The safe house had held. The evidence was safe. The battle for truth had survived its first major test. But outside, the storm of Singh's retaliation was far from over, the war was only beginning.

CHAPTER : 11

REGROUP AND RETALIATE

Dawn broke over Pune in a muted haze, rain-soaked streets reflecting the soft light. Inside the safe house, the team moved in silence, the adrenaline of the night's siege still pulsing through their veins. Broken furniture and splintered wood littered the floor, reminders of the chaos that had raged just hours before.

Avni surveyed the room, mind already calculating the next steps. The first strike had been repelled, but Singh was far from defeated. If they didn't act decisively now, the syndicate would regroup and escalate further. The evidence had survived the night, but public exposure alone would not be enough, they needed leverage, strategy, and precision.

Jamkar, still alert, surveyed the street through a narrow slit in the shutters. "They'll test us again tonight. Singh doesn't back down when embarrassed. He'll come with more, heavier, and smarter," he warned.

Rakesh and Sunil worked quickly to repair and reinforce makeshift barricades. Every board replaced, every door lock double-checked, every potential weak point strengthened. Avni gave precise instructions, assigning tasks with a calm authority that belied her fatigue.

Kavita booted up her laptop, reviewing the partial upload of the third leak. It was already circulating online, sparking debates, outrage, and the beginnings of an official inquiry. Yet, Avni knew the syndicate's influence ran deep, this was only the first ripple of a larger storm they had to navigate carefully.

Avni addressed the team. "We've survived the first wave, but survival isn't enough. Tonight, we plan our offensive. We hit Singh's network where it hurts, financially, politically, publicly. We make him react, not us. But precision is critical. One misstep, and everything falls."

The group nodded, a shared determination passing between them. Outside, the city was quiet for now, but Avni could feel the tension like a living thing. The battle for truth in Pune had entered a new phase.

Avni laid a fresh sheet on the table and drew three concentric rings, public pressure, legal challenge, and financial disruption, each with corresponding tactics pinned beneath. "We'll move on three fronts," she said, her voice steady. "Kavita and I keep the narrative tight in the press. Jamkar coordinates limited, credible leaks to law enforcement sympathetic to the cause. Rakesh and Anil will hit the financial threads, paper trails and palpably verifiable transactions. Sunil and Raghav, you'll work on operational corroboration: manifests, courier testimony, and timing logs."

Kavita tapped keys, already composing precise narratives that framed the scandal in human terms: betrayed youth programs, ruined careers, and institutional betrayal. The goal was to make the public care enough to demand action while denying Singh easy legal counters. "We expose facts that can't be spun," she said. "No hyperbole, just documents and testimony they can't refute."

Jamkar added the law- enforcement dimension. "I have contacts willing to receive material under seal. If we present the recorder and bank logs to the right magistrate, we can get protective orders for witnesses and a court- sanctioned investigation. It forces the board's hand and slows Singh's legal countermoves."

Rakesh and Anil cross-checked the timeline, flagging three transfers worth prioritizing for immediate forensic audit. Those transfers, they agreed, would form the core evidence for asset freezes and injunctions. Avni assigned deadlines and safe drop protocols: physical handoffs in daylight, multiple witnesses, and parallel backups hidden off- site.

Practicalities followed: contingency safe houses, a rotation of decoys for public appearances, and a signal system if anyone felt endangered. They scheduled encrypted, in- person handovers with the legal adviser and arranged for a trusted national journalist to hold the initial sealed affidavit until simultaneous publication.

As the plan took shape, Avni felt the familiar, dangerous exhilaration, this was more than exposé work; it was a coordinated counteroffensive to dismantle a machine of corruption. The stakes were higher than ever, but now, so was their readiness.

Avni set the timeline in motion. By midmorning, Rakesh and Anil were en route to a neutral notary with sealed copies of the prioritized transfers, each accompanied by two witnesses and a notarized chain- of- custody form. Sunil coordinated with Raghav to secure additional courier manifests and cross- reference vehicle numbers; each newly matched piece of evidence tightened the legal noose.

Kavita arranged an exclusive embargoed briefing with a national paper's legal desk, an outlet large enough to make a public dent but prudent enough to hold the story until the legal motions were filed. The plan: publish immediately after magistrate filings and protective orders were served, making it difficult for Singh to bury the narrative behind defamation suits or procedural maneuvers. Timing, Avni insisted, would be their best defense.

Jamkar worked quietly, calling in favors. He scheduled a covert meeting with a magistrate known for impartiality and integrity, one who could accept sealed evidence and, if the paper showed probable cause, issue urgent protective measures. The inspector's voice was low but urgent on the phone: this case needed to be framed as public corruption threatening minors and the integrity of sport; it couldn't be dismissed as internecine sport politics.

Avni checked on the team's welfare between tasks, meals, short rests, and briefings so that panic didn't erode discipline. The safe house would remain their operational hub for now; evac routes were rehearsed again, and contingency funds were allocated for immediate relocations. She felt the team's confidence strengthen with each verified handoff.

By late afternoon, the first documents were in the magistrate's hands and the notary stamps glinted like small, stubborn victories. The machinery of law and public opinion had begun to turn in their favor, and for the first time since the bat had been found, Avni allowed herself a guarded hope that the syndicate's days of impunity might finally be numbered.

The magistrate's chambers smelled of old paper and quiet authority. Avni watched from a discreet distance as Jamkar slipped the sealed packet across the judge's desk, hand- stamped affidavits, notarized transfers, and a copy of the recorder Jamkar had produced. The magistrate, a stern woman with a reputation for cutting through legal fog, skimmed the documents with experienced eyes.

Within hours, the wheels began to turn. The court issued a temporary order: immediate preservation of digital logs, notification to banking compliance units to freeze suspicious transfers, and most crucially, protective measures for named witnesses. The judge's directive was clinical and precise, designed to deny the syndicate the usual playbook of delays and intimidation. Avni felt the weight of relief and urgency in equal measure; legal validation had moved the fight out of rumor and into enforceable law.

News of the court action leaked quickly. Newspapers amplified the message; politicians who had been complacent now issued cautious calls for inquiry. Sponsors publicly threatened to suspend funding pending investigations. Singh's carefully cultivated calm shifted into contained fury. He convened emergency meetings, and his legal team mobilized instantly, filings, injunction threats, and public statements accusing unnamed journalists of "malicious fabrication."

Inside the safe house, the atmosphere crackled. Victory tasted immediate but fragile. Rakesh and Anil braced for reprisals; their movement schedules tightened. Kavita coordinated with national outlets to align publication times with legal notices, ensuring maximum protection through public scrutiny. Jamkar monitored police channels, watching for any sign that official enforcement might be compromised.

Avni allowed herself one small but deliberate breath. The law had provided a new shield; the public had provided a new lever. Yet the syndicate still had resources, reach and retaliation methods that could bypass courts. The battle had shifted to a higher plane: legal strategy, public pressure, and the race to secure more testimony before Singh could counterattack. The next phase would demand equal parts caution and audacity.

By evening, the safe house hummed with controlled activity. Every member of Avni's team had a clearly defined role, their movements synchronized like clockwork. The storm from the previous night had subsided, leaving the streets of Pune wet and silent, a deceptive calm that Avni knew could conceal any number of threats.

Rakesh monitored communications and local traffic, scanning for unusual vehicles or patterns that could signal Singh's reconnaissance teams. Sunil double-checked the relocated evidence, ensuring all copies were accounted for and cross-verified. Kavita coordinated with journalists, confirming that the third leak would be released simultaneously with the formal legal notice, guaranteeing maximum impact.

Avni gathered the team for a quick briefing. "Singh will not sit idle. He's unpredictable, ruthless, and connected. He may try to infiltrate or intimidate our sources. We anticipate surveillance, interference with communications, and attempts at legal harassment. Our defense must be proactive."

Jamkar added, "We can expect direct provocations. Some men will act without orders, testing reactions. Don't engage unless necessary; contain and observe, report immediately. The less we reveal about our positions, the longer we maintain control."

The group reviewed contingency plans. Safe houses were mapped in a staggered sequence across Pune, signals were rehearsed for emergencies, and the team rehearsed a rapid evacuation route through back alleys and concealed passages. Every variable had a countermeasure; every risk was catalogued.

As night fell, Avni allowed herself a brief glance at the partially uploaded leak. The narrative was reaching the public: board officials under scrutiny, financial manipulations exposed, and witness testimonies surfacing. Singh's empire was beginning to crack, though he remained a formidable adversary.

The team settled into tense vigilance. The battle for truth was far from over, but tonight, they had reclaimed the initiative. Outside, shadows moved silently along rain-slick streets, a reminder that the fight had entered its deadliest phase yet.

The first signs of Singh's counterattack came subtly. By late night, Avni noticed unusual activity around key witnesses. A courier tasked with delivering supporting documents reported being followed; a minor technical glitch in the encrypted upload system suggested tampering attempts. These were not random, they were deliberate, targeted, and calculated to intimidate or compromise.

Avni called an emergency team meeting. "They're probing our network, testing our sources. We can't assume safety anywhere outside this house," she said. Her voice was calm but edged with urgency. "Each leak, each witness, is a potential target. We must anticipate and neutralize threats before they materialize."

Jamkar outlined his plan. "We split protective duties. I'll secure witnesses with legal cover and discreet relocation. Rakesh monitors their movements remotely. Sunil ensures evidence isn't compromised, and Kavita maintains secure lines to press outlets. Every action must be verifiable, every movement trackable."

Avni reviewed additional options. Safe houses were activated in rotation to throw off tailing, burner phones assigned for all communication, and digital decoys prepared to mislead any intercept attempts. Every team member memorized alternate routes and rendezvous points.

Outside, Singh's operatives began to pressure the first witnesses. One, a former board clerk, noticed a suspicious black SUV following him across Pune. Another, responsible for courier deliveries, found a note slipped under the door, anonymous, menacing, and precise in its threat.

Inside the safe house, Avni's team acted quickly. Protective measures were implemented immediately, new contingency plans deployed, and encrypted communications doubled. Avni knew the syndicate's reach extended far and wide; the challenge now was to outmaneuver a ruthless opponent without revealing their own positions.

The night had shifted from reactive defense to calculated counter-surveillance. Singh's first wave of psychological pressure had begun, and Avni's team had only hours to respond before the next escalation.

By the early hours of the morning, Avni had finalized her offensive strategy. Singh's syndicate relied on fear and coordination, but Avni knew their arrogance was also their weakness. A carefully timed series of exposures and legal pressure could force them into mistakes.

"Here's the plan," she said, gathering the team around the battered table. "We hit their financial trails first. Rakesh and Anil will leak verified transaction anomalies to banking authorities under protective cover. Kavita and I release the corroborated stories to the national press simultaneously. Jamkar and Sunil will monitor for any violent retaliation or attempts to intercept witnesses. Timing is everything. We give them no opportunity to consolidate or intimidate."

Rakesh nodded, double- checking the encrypted files. "The transfers we flagged last week are airtight. Once submitted, the banks have no choice but to freeze assets temporarily. That buys us leverage."

Kavita's fingers hovered over her keyboard, eyes scanning each document. "The narrative is precise. Facts only, no opinion, no speculation. Singh can't argue against these pieces without implicating himself further."

Jamkar added, "I've coordinated with trusted officers. Protective orders for witnesses will be issued immediately after submission. They'll have no room to interfere physically without alerting law enforcement."

Avni felt a surge of controlled adrenaline. Every variable was accounted for, every contingency mapped. The offensive would be executed in three coordinated strikes: financial, legal, and public exposure.

The team split into their roles, each member moving with disciplined efficiency. Avni monitored every communication line, every encrypted upload, and every movement in the city that could indicate syndicate response.

For the first time in weeks, she felt the momentum shift. Singh had underestimated them once, and now, carefully, deliberately, they were going to turn the tables. The war for truth in Pune had entered its most dangerous, decisive phase.

The city streets of Pune remained eerily quiet as the first phase of Avni's offensive began. Rakesh and Anil submitted the verified transaction anomalies to the banking authorities through discreet channels, their movements synchronized to avoid detection. Each submission was meticulously logged, creating a paper trail Singh could not erase.

Inside the safe house, Kavita activated the press release. Carefully structured and evidence-backed, the stories began circulating across national outlets. Headlines flashed: "Cricket Board Corruption Exposed: Financial and Ethical Breaches Revealed," accompanied by documents and testimonies. Public outrage built rapidly, amplified by social media shares and political commentators picking up the narrative.

Jamkar monitored the streets, alert for any unusual activity. Within hours, Singh's operatives began reacting. Vehicles appeared at a distance, circling neighborhoods linked to witnesses. Messages, subtle threats, and attempts to intercept couriers confirmed the syndicate's awareness of the unfolding offensive.

Avni moved among her team, issuing precise instructions. "Maintain position, but observe all patterns. Any move from Singh's men is intelligence. Do not engage unless unavoidable. Let them expose themselves."

Sunil cross-referenced updates from Rakesh with the witness locations, ensuring every individual remained in protected zones. Every step of the syndicate's response was mapped, giving Avni leverage and insight into their chain of command.

By midnight, the combined effect of legal filings, public exposure, and financial disruptions began to force cracks. Singh convened emergency meetings with his lieutenants, arguments flaring, tensions rising. Panic was showing in their precision, and Avni's team used this opportunity to tighten security, prepare for the next strike, and consolidate the evidence.

The battle was no longer just defensive. Pune's cricketing underworld was exposed to daylight, and Avni had taken the initiative. Singh had been forced onto the back foot, but the fight was far from over.

Singh's fury became palpable. By the early hours, intelligence confirmed that he was mobilizing a more aggressive counterattack. The first wave of operatives had already been compromised by Avni's strategy; now he was sending specialists, men trained to infiltrate, intimidate, and eliminate high-value targets.

Inside the safe house, Avni convened the team. "They've escalated," she said, voice steady but firm. "Expect targeted strikes against our witnesses and couriers. Their goal is simple: disrupt, intimidate, and buy time to regain control. We anticipate patterns and exploit weaknesses. Discipline and coordination are our shield."

Rakesh updated the maps of witness locations and routes, marking surveillance points and potential ambush zones. Sunil ensured all evidence remained protected, moving any high-risk documents into secondary, undisclosed caches. Kavita double-checked press schedules, confirming that the release would continue uninterrupted regardless of Singh's maneuvers.

Jamkar coordinated protective teams for witnesses, deploying decoys and rotating safe houses in unpredictable patterns. He emphasized vigilance: even a minor oversight could result in compromised testimony or worse. Every operative knew the stakes.

Outside, vehicles with tinted windows moved methodically through Pune, attempting to track couriers and witnesses. Singh's men were skilled, but the psychological pressure of the leak and the freezing of financial channels slowed their coordination.

Avni reviewed the partial media impact. Public outrage was growing, investigative journalists were calling for hearings, and political figures were signaling support. Singh had to act quickly, but every move carried risk.

"This is the moment to force errors," Avni told the team. "We defend, we monitor, we exploit. He cannot regain control without exposing himself further. Stay sharp, stay coordinated, and protect the evidence. Everything else follows."

The city outside was silent, but the storm was far from over. Singh's desperation was about to collide with Avni's meticulous preparation.

By late night, the tension reached its peak. Singh's desperate operatives tried multiple infiltration tactics, fake couriers, anonymous tips, and shadowing witnesses, but Avni's team had anticipated nearly every move. Each attempt to breach their network was met with calculated countermeasures, leaving Singh frustrated and exposed.

Inside the safe house, Avni coordinated the team with precision. Rakesh monitored street-level activity, signaling every suspicious approach. Jamkar remained in constant contact with the magistrate's office, ensuring that legal protections for witnesses were enforced without delay. Sunil moved evidence between hidden compartments, while Kavita managed live updates for the press, keeping public attention sharply focused on Singh's wrongdoing.

Suddenly, a call from one of the couriers reported a near-abduction attempt. Avni's heart raced, but she remained composed. "Follow the diversion protocol," she instructed. "Reroute immediately and maintain radio silence. Do not engage unless cornered."

Outside, black SUVs disappeared into the rainy streets, frustrated by the decoys and unpredictable movements of Avni's team. Singh's operatives realized their own errors too late, every failed move further weakened their leverage and exposed them to legal consequences.

By dawn, a pattern had emerged. Singh's network was splintering under the combined pressure of media exposure, financial freezes, and law enforcement oversight. The once seemingly invincible syndicate had been forced into defensive postures, scrambling to salvage influence while public scrutiny mounted.

Avni allowed herself a measured nod of satisfaction. The team had survived, adapted, and executed their counteroffensive flawlessly. Yet she knew the fight was not over, Singh's resources remained vast, and his next move would be desperate and potentially lethal.

The siege had shifted from reactive defense to strategic dominance. For now, Avni had gained the initiative and with it, the chance to finally bring Singh's empire to justice.

CHAPTER : 12

- - - - - - - - - - - -

CONSOLIDATING THE EVIDENCE

The morning sun broke over Pune, casting a muted glow on rain-slicked streets. Inside the safe house, the team moved with purposeful efficiency. The previous night's siege had ended, but the work was far from complete. Avni knew that surviving the first assault was only a step, the ultimate goal was to dismantle Singh's network entirely.

Avni gathered the team around the table. "Singh is scrambling. The financial channels are frozen, the media is exposing him, and law enforcement is alerted. But he still has resources, influence, and desperate men. Our next step is consolidation. Every document, every transaction, every testimony must be verified, cross-referenced, and ready for legal action."

Rakesh spread digital and physical copies of bank statements, highlighting suspicious transfers and patterns. "We've confirmed these three major channels," he said. "If we can trace the final beneficiary accounts, we can complete the chain of accountability."

Sunil checked courier logs and witness reports, making sure each handoff had a documented time and location. "We can correlate these with bank transfers and board approvals. Everything lines up, but gaps remain, some minor, some critical."

Kavita opened the encrypted drafts for media publications. "The story is growing organically. Public pressure is mounting. Politicians are being forced to act. But the narrative must stay tight; no leaks beyond the plan, or Singh will try to spin it."

Jamkar added, "I've scheduled discreet witness interviews today. Protective orders are in place. Any deviation could compromise the chain of evidence. We have to be methodical."

Avni leaned back, eyes scanning her team. They were exhausted, but focused. Every move from this point onward needed precision. One misstep could undo weeks of planning and risk everything, lives, evidence, and the hard-earned momentum.

The day's mission was clear: consolidate, verify, and prepare for the final strike against Singh's empire. Failure was not an option.

Avni divided the team into specialized units. Rakesh focused on tracing the last financial connections, offshore accounts, shell corporations, and intermediaries used to funnel illicit funds. Each discovery tightened the net around Singh's operations, providing actionable leads for law enforcement.

Sunil and Jamkar coordinated witness interviews, ensuring every statement was notarized and cross-referenced with physical and digital evidence. They reviewed CCTV footage, courier logs, and transaction timestamps, building a chronological web that left no room for ambiguity. Every detail, however minor, mattered in a case that could collapse under scrutiny if improperly documented.

Kavita worked on the media narrative, carefully scripting follow-ups to the previous leaks. Headlines and stories were prepared in advance, ready to be released in sync with key legal filings. The aim was to maintain constant public pressure while avoiding gaps that Singh could exploit for counter-narratives or disinformation.

Avni monitored each team's progress, coordinating the flow of information between units. Her mind was always three steps ahead, anticipating potential challenges, ensuring redundancies, and maintaining operational security. The smallest oversight could compromise months of work.

By mid-afternoon, Rakesh had identified the final link: a minor shell company used to funnel bribes to influential politicians and board officials. The paper trail was labyrinthine, but meticulous cross-checking confirmed the connection. This was the missing piece, the keystone in their legal strategy.

Avni's pulse quickened. With this final connection, the team could assemble an airtight case. The battle for truth was nearing its climax, and every subsequent action would determine whether Singh's empire would crumble or survive another day.

Avni convened the team in the war room, the walls covered in maps, timelines, and cross-referenced documents. Every piece of evidence was laid out, every connection visualized. "This is it," she said, voice calm but resolute. "The final link is verified. If we act now, Singh's network will face an undeniable collapse."

Rakesh pointed to the shell company on the map. "All transactions converge here. From this single entity, we can trace payments to board officials, politicians, and intermediaries. Once the authorities have this chain, Singh's influence evaporates."

Sunil and Jamkar reviewed witness statements and CCTV logs again, confirming that each deposition corresponded exactly with the financial data. Any discrepancies could be challenged, so meticulous double-checking was essential. "All corroboration is complete," Jamkar reported. "We're airtight."

Kavita coordinated the media release schedule. "We align publication with the legal filings. The first wave exposes corruption, the second reveals the political connections, and the third emphasizes the personal testimonies of whistleblowers. The public narrative will leave Singh little room to maneuver."

Avni outlined the operation in precise detail. Rakesh and Anil would submit the verified financial trail to the magistrate's office, ensuring protective measures for all involved. Jamkar would coordinate real-time security for witnesses, while Sunil oversaw the integrity of physical and digital evidence. Kavita would time the media release to coincide with the magistrate's verification, maximizing impact.

The team absorbed each instruction, understanding the stakes. This was the culmination of weeks of investigation, threats, and near-fatal confrontations. One coordinated action could dismantle Singh's empire or, if mishandled, provide him a chance to retaliate.

Avni took a deep breath, feeling the weight of responsibility. Tonight, strategy would meet execution and the city of Pune would bear witness to the reckoning.

They moved like a single unit as dusk fell. Rakesh and Anil set off with sealed affidavits and notarized transfer chains, each envelope carried by separate couriers to different magistrate branches, redundancy to prevent a single point of failure. Jamkar coordinated the handoffs, staying in constant, silent contact with the court liaison; his voice over the burner was low and efficient, the language of someone used to moving evidence through bureaucracy without fanfare.

Sunil and Raghav took responsibility for the physical archives: manifests, envelopes, and the original notebook pages. They moved them into a rented locker facility under assumed names and double- wrapped drives into inconspicuous containers. Nothing remained in one place long enough to be targeted. Avni supervised every placement, confirming serial numbers and cross- checking catalogues until each item was logged in triplicate.

Kavita prepared the narrative scaffolding: an advance brief to the national desk, a prioritized list of documents to release, and precise headlines that would leave no wiggle room for legal ambiguity. Timing was surgical, the press release would follow the magistrate's acknowledgment by minutes, not hours, collapsing the window in which Singh's lawyers could file obstructionary suits.

Before departure, Avni gathered the team for a final check. They reviewed signals, escape routes, and emergency contacts, then sealed their phones, keeping only burners live for essential coordination. The air was taut; everyone understood that the coming hours would define the campaign's success.

As the magistrate's office confirmed receipt of the final packet, Avni felt a hard, relieved clarity. The legal machinery had been engaged; the media would amplify it; and the people at the center of the conspiracy had nowhere left to hide. Outside, Pune's sidewalks glowed from recent rain, the city waiting, unaware that by dawn its cricketing institutions might be irrevocably altered.

At dawn, the first official ripples began. The magistrate issued interim orders: immediate forensic audits of flagged accounts, temporary freezes on several corporate bank records, and most importantly, an order to secure witness protection for those named in the filings. The court's decisive language removed much of the syndicate's usual legal smokescreen; it was no longer easy to bury the story in procedural delays.

Kavita's team published the coordinated release exactly as planned. Headlines across national and regional papers named the shell companies, quoted notarized affidavits, and reproduced redacted but damning transaction chains. Television panels debated the implications; anchors repeated the magistrate's orders verbatim. Across Pune, sports clubs, sponsors, and civic groups could no longer pretend ignorance.

Singh's camp reacted predictably and visibly. His legal team filed an emergency petition seeking to quash the magistrate's order, while his public relations team flooded media channels with obfuscation and counteraccusations. But now every assertion they made was subject to immediate cross- check against notarized documents and independent banking verifications. The media, armed with evidence, pushed back; public sentiment turned from speculation to outrage.

Meanwhile, Jamkar moved to coordinate police protection for high- risk witnesses. Assigned officers arrived at safe houses and transport hubs; phone lines were monitored; decoy routes were established. Rakesh confirmed that two of the previously opaque beneficiary accounts had been frozen by morning; the banking compliance unit had not only acted but had begun tracing outgoing transfers.

Avni watched the cascade with a mix of exhaustion and guarded triumph. The plan was working, and yet she knew this phase demanded vigilance. Legal battles, political maneuvering, and private vendettas would attempt to blunt the momentum. For now, though, the evidence was secure, the public was watching, and Singh's empire had been forced onto the defensive. The next moves would determine whether justice would follow exposure, or whether the syndicate would survive, battered but intact.

By late morning, the full scale of Singh's desperation became evident. Insider sources within his network reported urgent meetings, arguments breaking out among his lieutenants, and hurried attempts to move untraceable assets. Panic was setting in, a direct result of the legal and media onslaught Avni had orchestrated.

Avni convened her team again. "They're scrambling," she said. "But we can't assume this ends here. Expect attempts to intimidate witnesses, manipulate minor legal technicalities, or even target couriers. Every move must be precise, documented, and protected."

Rakesh updated the digital map, highlighting the frozen accounts, pending audits, and key board officials under scrutiny. Each verified connection tightened the net, leaving Singh with diminishing options. "He's reacting, not planning," Rakesh observed. "That's our advantage, he makes mistakes now, and we capitalize."

Jamkar confirmed witness protection protocols: rotations for safe houses, decoy travel routes, and round-the-clock monitoring. Even minor lapses could allow a skilled operative to intimidate or bribe key individuals, potentially unraveling the case. The stakes were higher than ever.

Sunil conducted a final cross-verification of physical and digital evidence, ensuring redundancy in case of sabotage or unforeseen attacks. Each folder, each encrypted drive, and each notarized page was meticulously accounted for.

Kavita synchronized the media rollout with legal filings, preparing follow-ups to highlight the growing scale of corruption. Public interest was now high, social media amplifying every document and testimony. Singh's window to counter the narrative was rapidly closing.

Avni observed the team's focus and precision, feeling a surge of cautious optimism. The battle for truth had shifted decisively; Singh's network was exposed, destabilized, and under scrutiny. Yet she knew the syndicate's final moves could still be dangerous and unpredictable. Every victory now required vigilance, strategy, and unwavering discipline.

By mid-afternoon, Avni began coordinating the final legal takedown. Every piece of evidence, every witness statement, every bank audit report had been compiled into a comprehensive dossier. This would form the foundation for criminal and civil proceedings against Singh and his network.

She gathered the team in the safe house, the room buzzing with tense anticipation. "This is the moment we consolidate everything," she said. "The magistrate has responded to initial filings. We submit the final package today, ensuring every transaction, every meeting, and every coercion attempt is documented. Singh's empire won't have room to maneuver, this is airtight."

Rakesh double-checked the documentation, confirming all digital signatures and notarized affidavits were properly formatted. "All trail points are verified," he said. "From offshore transfers to board approvals, nothing has been overlooked. This is the legal hammer."

Jamkar reviewed witness readiness. "Protective measures are in place. Interviews have been cross-checked and backed with evidence. Any attempt to intimidate or bribe will be immediately reportable to the court."

Sunil ensured that every physical artifact, from notebooks to courier logs, was properly cataloged and duplicated in secure offsite storage. Even if the syndicate managed to interfere in one location, a complete backup existed.

Kavita prepared press briefings to follow immediately after the magistrate received the final package. The goal was to maintain public pressure while preventing Singh from spinning a counter-narrative. Every headline, every release, was synchronized with court filings to maximize impact.

Avni looked around at her team. Fatigue was etched on their faces, but determination burned brighter. Today was the culmination of weeks of investigation, risk, and strategy. Singh's final exposure was imminent, and the city of Pune would soon witness the fall of a carefully hidden empire.

By late afternoon, the team was ready to execute the final submission. Avni oversaw the coordinated effort like a conductor leading a symphony, every movement, every handoff, and every document had a precise place in the operation.

Rakesh and Anil transported the notarized affidavits, digital transfer records, and supporting documentation to the magistrate's office via separate, secure routes. Each courier carried a copy with redundant verification protocols, ensuring that no single failure could compromise the evidence.

Jamkar coordinated real-time security. Witnesses were relocated to safe houses with decoys and rotation schedules, while mobile units monitored potential surveillance or interference attempts. Every intersection, alley, and route was mapped and double-checked for anomalies.

Inside the safe house, Sunil and Raghav prepared the final digital backups, encrypting them with multiple layers and distributing them across hidden cloud servers. Each copy was tied to verification logs, ensuring authenticity in case Singh attempted to dispute the material.

Kavita finalized media coordination. Press releases, pre-approved storylines, and headline graphics were queued to release immediately upon magistrate confirmation.

The aim was to collapse Singh's window for reactive spin and force him into a purely defensive position.

As Rakesh submitted the first package to the magistrate's desk, Avni's phone buzzed with confirmation from the second courier. Both had been successfully delivered, verified, and logged. The evidence was officially in judicial hands.

Avni allowed herself a brief, controlled exhale. The network's collapse had begun. Every layer of Singh's empire, from financial schemes to political influence, was now exposed to legal scrutiny, public oversight, and media amplification.

Outside, Pune moved obliviously beneath clouds and faint evening light. Inside the safe house, the quiet hum of machines and determined activity marked a new phase. Singh's era of hidden corruption was ending, and Avni's calculated strategy was about to bring the final reckoning.

By nightfall, the first waves of impact rippled through Singh's network. Banks froze suspect accounts, auditors began investigations, and board officials who had previously ignored the signs were forced into urgent explanations. Public and media scrutiny intensified, leaving the syndicate scrambling for control.

Kavita monitored social media trends and press coverage. Hashtags detailing the scandal trended nationally within hours. News channels highlighted the magistrate's orders alongside excerpts from notarized evidence, making it impossible for Singh to spin the narrative without contradicting hard facts. Public outrage grew with each passing hour, and influential figures began calling for immediate accountability.

Inside the safe house, Jamkar received multiple reports of panicked operatives. Vehicles tailing witnesses had been identified and documented, and decoy strategies had successfully diverted several attempts to intimidate key individuals. Singh's men were reacting, but their moves were predictable under Avni's meticulous surveillance.

Rakesh confirmed that all remaining financial trails were now under forensic review. "Every shell account, every transfer, every suspicious ledger entry is logged. Singh's financial mobility is effectively frozen," he reported.

Sunil double-checked the backup copies, ensuring that no digital or physical evidence could be compromised. "Everything is duplicated and stored securely offsite. Any attempt to destroy originals will fail," he said.

Avni gathered the team for a quick briefing. "The network is destabilized, but this isn't the end," she reminded them. "Expect legal counter-moves, political interference, and possibly physical intimidation. Our task now is to maintain pressure, protect witnesses, and ensure every piece of evidence is presented in court intact. One slip could undo everything."

Despite exhaustion, the team felt the surge of accomplishment. For the first time, Singh's empire seemed vulnerable. The momentum had shifted; the syndicate was reacting, and Avni's strategy was forcing their mistakes.

Singh, cornered and furious, convened a late-night emergency meeting with his closest lieutenants. Tempers flared as blame circulated, operatives had failed, transfers were frozen, and public exposure was rampant. Desperation replaced strategy.

Avni monitored the situation through multiple intelligence channels. The syndicate's panic was predictable, but dangerous. Singh would attempt a high-risk move, likely targeting witnesses, couriers, or even exploiting legal loopholes to delay proceedings. She knew they had only hours to preempt his next strike.

Jamkar intensified protective measures. Witnesses were moved to secondary safe houses, decoy convoys ran timed rotations, and digital communication channels were fortified against interception. Every team member doubled down on vigilance, understanding that a single lapse could be fatal.

Rakesh and Anil focused on the financial front, providing real-time updates on any sudden transfers or attempts to bypass freezing orders. Their monitoring revealed small, hurried maneuvers, temporary accounts and shell intermediaries, already blocked by the banking authorities. Singh's attempts to regain liquidity were failing.

Kavita prepared for the final press amplification. "Every legal confirmation, every notarized affidavit, every frozen account will be paired with public coverage. We'll maintain a continuous pressure window. Singh's mistakes are now being broadcast in real time," she said.

Avni addressed the team, her voice calm yet resolute. "Tonight, Singh is desperate. He will act recklessly. We stay disciplined, maintain our layers of protection, and execute the final consolidation. Every piece of evidence is verified. Every witness is protected. Nothing is left to chance."

As darkness deepened over Pune, the city seemed calm, but within the hidden corridors of power and crime, Singh's desperation set the stage for the climactic confrontation. Avni and her team were ready. The final reckoning was imminent.

CHAPTER : 13

THE FINAL CONFRONTATION

The first rays of dawn filtered through the dusty windows of Pune's magistrate office, but inside, tension was electric. Avni and her team arrived early, dossiers in hand, ready to witness the culmination of weeks of planning, surveillance, and relentless risk. Today would determine whether Singh's empire fell or survived.

Rakesh carried the final financial compilations, cross-referenced with notarized affidavits. Each page was meticulously verified, every transaction mapped to a corresponding witness account or official document. There could be no error, Singh's legal team would pounce on even a minor discrepancy.

Sunil ensured the physical and digital evidence backups were secure, encrypted, and cataloged. In the adjacent room, Jamkar coordinated with court officers, arranging protective measures for the witnesses who would testify or submit statements. Decoy vehicles and safe routes had been confirmed, leaving no openings for sabotage or intimidation.

Kavita readied the media team. The press was under strict embargo, scheduled to release stories in exact alignment with the court filings. The objective was simple: expose Singh's corruption in full view of the public, leaving him no maneuvering space, legal or otherwise.

Avni paused for a moment, surveying her team. Exhaustion marked their faces, but determination burned brightly. Weeks of close calls, threats, and meticulous planning had brought them here. She felt a flicker of apprehension, Singh was dangerous, and his desperation made him unpredictable, but it was tempered by confidence in the evidence, in the legal machinery, and in her team's discipline.

As the magistrate called them into the chamber, Avni straightened, shoulders squared. The room was quiet except for the rustle of papers and the low hum of fluorescent lights. Today, strategy would meet execution. Today, the truth would confront a man who had long believed himself untouchable.

The courtroom was a mixture of tension and subdued chaos. Singh sat at the defense table, flanked by his legal team, his expression a mask of controlled fury. He scanned the room, eyes narrowing as Avni and her team entered with the compiled evidence. For the first time, he seemed aware of the scale of exposure he faced.

Avni stepped forward, her dossier clutched firmly. She had rehearsed every detail countless times, memorized every connection, every transaction, and every witness statement. "Your honor," she began, voice steady and authoritative, "we submit a comprehensive package of evidence detailing systematic corruption, financial manipulation, and intimidation orchestrated by Mr. Vikram Singh and his network. Each document is verified, notarized, and cross-referenced for accuracy."

The magistrate, a stern and meticulous figure, examined the submissions carefully. Pages were reviewed, bank trails verified, and witness affidavits checked against physical and digital evidence. Singh's lawyers immediately objected, claiming procedural errors, but every objection was countered by meticulously prepared documentation and time-stamped verifications.

Rakesh presented the financial trail, pointing to shell companies, offshore accounts, and suspicious transfers. Sunil displayed encrypted backups and original logs, demonstrating authenticity and redundancy. Jamkar confirmed that all witnesses were under protective orders, ready to testify or submit statements without fear of retaliation.

Outside, the media buzzed, tipped off by Kavita's scheduled alerts. News channels broadcast initial confirmations, highlighting the magnitude of Singh's exposure. Public pressure was immediate, forcing even political allies to distance themselves subtly.

Avni watched Singh closely. His composure was fraying, tiny twitches betraying panic. The carefully constructed empire he had built on fear, influence, and manipulation was now under relentless scrutiny, and he had nowhere to hide.

Singh's lawyers rose in unison, their motions deliberate and practiced. "Your honor," one began, voice dripping with feigned confidence, "we contend that several of these documents were obtained unlawfully. Some witness statements were coerced, and certain financial records lack proper chain-of-custody verification. We request dismissal or at least a pause to examine procedural flaws."

Avni's pulse quickened, but her composure remained unshaken. She anticipated this exact maneuver. Calmly, she interjected, "Your honor, every document submitted is notarized and time-stamped. Witness statements were voluntarily provided under legal protection. Chain-of-custody logs exist for every transfer and handoff. We have multiple redundant verifications, physical, digital, and third-party confirmations. Procedural integrity is absolute."

The magistrate studied the submissions with meticulous attention. Singh's legal team pressed on, attempting psychological tactics, whispered comments, pointed glances, subtle intimidation, but each move was anticipated. Jamkar maintained his presence beside key witnesses, ready to enforce protective measures, while Rakesh ensured the magistrate had immediate access to any supporting financial evidence requested.

Kavita monitored live media feeds, noting public reactions. Every objection from Singh's team was countered by factual reporting and visual documentation, leaving the public, and even political observers, leaning toward the prosecution's side. Social media amplified the narrative: hashtags like #SinghExposed and #JusticeForCricket trended nationwide.

Singh's face betrayed frustration, his composed veneer cracking. He knew that even a temporary legal maneuver could not erase the avalanche of evidence meticulously compiled and strategically timed for maximum exposure. Every attempt to delay or discredit the case was met with airtight documentation, leaving him trapped in a tightening web of accountability.

Avni allowed herself a measured breath. Singh's desperation was escalating, but she was ready. Every step they had taken led to this confrontation, and the final collapse of his empire was now within reach.

The magistrate leaned forward, reviewing the submissions with a keen, methodical eye. Each page of notarized affidavits, every digital ledger, and the complete bank trail was examined in meticulous detail. Singh's lawyers attempted to interject repeatedly, citing procedural technicalities, but the magistrate raised a hand, signaling patience yet firm authority.

Avni observed silently, noting the subtle shift in Singh's demeanor. His jaw tightened, fingers tapping nervously on the table. The once confident and untouchable figure now faced scrutiny that could not be sidestepped, spun, or manipulated. The evidence was comprehensive, undeniable, and strategically overwhelming.

Rakesh pointed to critical entries, emphasizing the flow of illicit transactions from shell companies to political intermediaries. “Every transfer is timestamped and corroborated by multiple sources,” he explained. “Any attempt to dispute these records can be independently verified.”

Sunil added, “Physical evidence, courier logs, and digital backups exist at separate, secured locations. Even if originals were compromised, which they are not, the redundant systems maintain full verification.”

Jamkar subtly checked on the witnesses present, confirming their confidence in the protective measures. Their presence underscored the strength of the case; every statement was independently backed and legally protected, making intimidation attempts ineffective.

Kavita’s media team awaited her signal. The synchronized release of public updates would coincide with the magistrate’s confirmation, amplifying pressure and leaving Singh’s network minimal room for maneuver.

Finally, the magistrate spoke, voice deliberate and calm. “The submissions appear comprehensive and procedurally sound. Preliminary review indicates the evidence is credible and verifiable. Immediate measures for investigation, audit, and protective enforcement will be enacted.”

Singh’s face drained of color. The room’s atmosphere shifted, legal dominance had been established, and the web of accountability tightened around him. Avni felt a surge of controlled triumph; the first decisive step in dismantling the empire had succeeded.

Singh's composure finally broke. His legal team exchanged anxious glances as he slammed a fist on the table, voice low but trembling with fury. "This isn't over," he hissed, trying to intimidate the magistrate and cast doubt on the evidence. But the weight of meticulous documentation, notarized affidavits, and digital verification left his threats hollow.

Avni remained calm, her presence commanding. She could feel the shift, the tide had turned. Every precaution, every double-checked procedure, every strategically timed media release had cornered Singh, leaving him scrambling. The once untouchable figure was now on the defensive.

Rakesh briefed the magistrate on the final financial trail. "These are verified offshore accounts linked directly to shell corporations and intermediaries associated with Mr. Singh. Every transfer has supporting documentation, corroborated by independent witnesses."

Sunil displayed the secured physical evidence, ensuring the magistrate could confirm authenticity. Jamkar confirmed that protective measures were fully in place, keeping witnesses secure against any intimidation attempts. Kavita coordinated a real-time press release, amplifying the case nationwide and ensuring Singh's network could not manipulate public perception.

Outside the courtroom, news of the magistrate's acknowledgment spread quickly. Social media exploded with coverage, hashtags trending across the country. Public sentiment was overwhelmingly against Singh, pressuring political allies to distance themselves and signaling to the syndicate that legal, financial, and social pressure was closing in.

Singh attempted one last legal maneuver, filing an urgent motion to delay proceedings, but the magistrate denied it, citing procedural integrity and the overwhelming corroboration of evidence. The message was clear: Singh's empire was exposed, his resources constrained, and his influence crumbling.

Avni allowed herself a brief moment of relief. The culmination of weeks of planning, risk, and strategy had brought them to this point. The final confrontation was far from over, but the advantage had decisively shifted. Singh's fall had begun.

As the courtroom proceedings continued, Singh's remaining operatives scrambled to salvage what little influence remained. Panic and confusion spread through his network. Key operatives abandoned secure locations, attempting to hide or sever ties, while junior members openly argued about the best way to respond to the unfolding crisis.

Avni monitored the situation closely. Every misstep by Singh's team was documented, every lapse in protocol recorded for the magistrate. "Their panic is our advantage," she told the team. "Stay focused, protect our witnesses, and ensure every move is verifiable. This is where the final collapse begins."

Rakesh provided an update on the financial front. "Attempts to reroute funds through minor intermediaries have been identified and frozen. The network's liquidity is crippled, and their fallback mechanisms are failing. Singh's empire has no room to maneuver."

Jamkar ensured witness security remained airtight. Each protected individual was moved, rotated, and monitored, leaving the syndicate unable to intimidate or manipulate testimony. Decoy convoys and backup safe houses minimized risk.

Sunil verified the integrity of all evidence, ensuring that digital and physical backups could withstand any sabotage attempts. Kavita prepared the next wave of media amplification, carefully timed stories highlighting the unfolding judicial review and the exposure of Singh's political connections.

Inside the courtroom, the magistrate began issuing interim measures: freezing additional accounts, scheduling immediate audits, and summoning implicated officials for questioning. Each order further constricted Singh's options.

Avni watched with controlled satisfaction. Singh's network, once confident and omnipotent, was unraveling in real time. Every deliberate step they had planned, the evidence gathering, witness protection, media coordination, was now converging to ensure the syndicate's irreversible collapse.

Outside, Pune's skyline remained calm, but within the corridors of power, a storm of accountability had begun, and there was no escape.

The courtroom was electric as the magistrate began summarizing the findings. Every piece of evidence, meticulously verified and cross-referenced, was acknowledged. Bank transfers, shell companies, notarized affidavits, and witness statements, all pointed to Singh's orchestrated corruption and criminal activity.

Singh's face, once a mask of control, now betrayed sheer panic. Legal maneuvers failed to mask the reality: his network was collapsing. The magistrate outlined immediate actions, freezing all linked accounts, enforcing protective measures for witnesses, and initiating formal audits of implicated entities.

Kavita coordinated the synchronized media release. Television anchors highlighted the magistrate's orders, social media platforms exploded with trending hashtags, and news portals published corroborated evidence excerpts. The public could see the magnitude of Singh's crimes. Sponsors, political allies, and affiliated organizations quickly distanced themselves, leaving the syndicate isolated.

Avni observed quietly, aware that the meticulous planning of weeks had brought this moment. Rakesh confirmed that all financial pathways were effectively frozen; Sunil verified that all physical and digital evidence remained secure and intact. Jamkar ensured witness safety, knowing that intimidation attempts would be futile against the coordinated protective measures.

Even Singh's most loyal lieutenants were beginning to turn against him, questioning his leadership and expressing fear of personal exposure. Panic and disarray replaced the once-disciplined syndicate, and the final cracks in the empire were unmistakable.

The magistrate's final words echoed through the chamber: "Given the evidence presented, immediate investigation, protective, and corrective measures are hereby authorized. Individuals implicated will face full legal accountability. The law will not tolerate obstruction or intimidation."

For Avni, the room's tension transformed into a quiet triumph. Singh's empire, built on manipulation, greed, and fear, was exposed. The city of Pune, and the nation, would witness the fall of a syndicate that had long operated in shadows.

Singh's attempts to salvage his empire were frantic but ineffective. Operatives tried to move funds through minor intermediaries, but Rakesh and the banking authorities intercepted every transaction. Social media amplified the magistrate's orders in real time, leaving no room for misinformation or spin.

Inside the courtroom, Singh's lawyers scrambled to file emergency petitions, but the magistrate denied them, citing the airtight verification of every piece of evidence. Each appeal only highlighted the magnitude of their client's exposure. Every failed maneuver further isolated Singh from political allies and sponsors, who distanced themselves to avoid public scrutiny.

Avni and her team maintained disciplined vigilance. Jamkar monitored witness locations, rotating decoy routes and ensuring that no one could be intimidated or silenced. Sunil confirmed that all physical and digital evidence remained secure and backed up offsite. Kavita coordinated ongoing media updates, releasing verified excerpts of bank statements, witness statements, and notarized affidavits to reinforce public awareness and maintain pressure.

Even Singh's closest lieutenants began to question their loyalty. Fear and uncertainty replaced obedience. Many discreetly began withdrawing support, seeking to protect themselves from inevitable legal consequences. Panic had replaced strategy in the syndicate, and chaos spread across its ranks.

By evening, Singh's options had dwindled. His financial channels were frozen, his political connections exposed, and his operatives scattered or defecting. Legal accountability was imminent, and public outrage ensured that no obstruction could succeed.

Avni felt a quiet surge of triumph but remained vigilant. The final phase was not just exposure, it was ensuring permanent dismantling of the network. Tonight, Singh's carefully constructed empire would crumble completely, and the syndicate's reign over Pune's cricketing and political circles would be broken.

By late night, Singh's empire was unraveling completely. Reports arrived of multiple arrests, board officials, shell company intermediaries, and minor operatives had been detained or questioned. Each arrest was accompanied by confiscation of documents, electronic devices, and financial records, further constricting Singh's control.

Avni coordinated with Jamkar to ensure witnesses were moved safely, anticipating any desperate attempt by the syndicate to retaliate. Decoy convoys, rotating safe houses, and constant surveillance made interference impossible. Sunil verified that all critical evidence remained secure and untampered.

Kavita released the final wave of media coverage: detailed narratives exposing the financial manipulations, political collusions, and intimidation tactics used by Singh's network. National and regional outlets amplified the coverage, and public discourse demanded immediate accountability. Sponsors, political allies, and influential figures were forced to take a stand, severing any remaining support.

Singh, increasingly isolated, attempted a last-minute appeal in court, but the magistrate's previous orders, combined with airtight documentation, rendered it futile. Legal avenues were exhausted, and the evidence was overwhelming. Panic replaced his former confidence, his once-commanding presence now reduced to anxious movements and whispered commands to operatives who no longer obeyed.

Rakesh confirmed that all financial networks were blocked, with audits underway for every account. The syndicate's ability to maneuver had been nullified; its cohesion disintegrated. Every move Singh could make was predictable and countered, leaving him exposed to the full force of law and public scrutiny.

Avni allowed herself a small, controlled smile. Weeks of meticulous investigation, planning, and risk had brought them here. Singh's empire, built on corruption, fear, and manipulation, was collapsing before their eyes. Pune, and the nation, would now witness the consequences of unchecked greed and deception.

By early morning, Singh's empire lay in ruins. Arrests had been made, accounts frozen, and influential allies had withdrawn support. The courts moved swiftly, audits were underway, and the witnesses' testimonies formed an unassailable record. The syndicate's cohesion was shattered, leaving Singh isolated and powerless.

Avni watched the news coverage unfold in real time. Headlines screamed of corruption, betrayal, and downfall. Social media amplified every verified detail, making it impossible for Singh to spin the narrative. The public outrage was palpable, ensuring that political interference could not delay justice.

Jamkar coordinated final witness relocations and security sweeps. Every individual connected to the investigation was protected, their statements verified and corroborated. Sunil confirmed that all backups, digital and physical, were safely stored, ensuring the integrity of evidence remained intact.

Kavita prepared the last press releases, highlighting the collective effort of investigative teams, whistleblowers, and legal authorities. The narrative focused not only on the downfall of Singh but also on accountability, transparency, and the triumph of truth over corruption.

Singh, now visibly broken, faced the magistrate alone. His attempts at delay, manipulation, and intimidation had failed entirely. The legal net, meticulously constructed by Avni and her team, left no room for maneuver. Every aspect of his network, financial, political, and operational, had been exposed and neutralized.

Avni felt a deep, quiet satisfaction. Weeks of strategy, risk, and relentless pursuit of truth had culminated in this moment. Pune's cricketing institutions, and the city itself, witnessed the fall of a man who had long believed himself untouchable.

As the final orders were read and Singh was escorted away, the sense of resolution was profound. Justice had prevailed, corruption had been exposed, and the city breathed a collective sigh of relief. For Avni and her team, the long battle had ended, but the story of vigilance and courage would linger far beyond this day.

CHAPTER : 14

AFTERMATH AND REFLECTION

The city of Pune woke to a transformed reality. Newspapers, television channels, and social media were flooded with coverage of Vikram Singh's arrest, the dismantling of his syndicate, and the exposure of corruption within the cricketing and political circles. Citizens discussed the events in cafes, offices, and public transport, grappling with a mixture of shock, relief, and vindication.

Avni stood by the window of her modest office, sipping her morning coffee. The exhaustion of weeks of relentless investigation weighed on her, but there was a sense of profound accomplishment. She reflected on the risks, threats, and countless sleepless nights that had led to this moment. The battle had been both external and internal, a test of courage, patience, and unwavering commitment to truth.

Rakesh entered with a stack of final reports. "All the financial audits are confirmed," he said. "The magistrate's orders are being enforced, and Singh's network is effectively neutralized. Even the minor operatives are either cooperating with authorities or facing legal consequences."

Sunil and Jamkar briefed her on witness settlements. Each individual had been safely relocated or provided legal protections. The redundancy of security measures had ensured no retaliatory actions from the remnants of Singh's network.

Kavita updated Avni on the media impact. The narrative had shifted from speculation to verified fact. Sponsors, political figures, and board members had publicly acknowledged the wrongdoing, pledging reforms and transparency. Public awareness had reached a peak, ensuring that the lessons of this scandal would linger.

Avni exhaled slowly, allowing herself a rare moment of relief. The story she had pursued relentlessly had not only revived her career but had also delivered justice. Pune had witnessed a reckoning, one built on courage, evidence, and perseverance. Yet, she knew vigilance was never over, the fight against corruption, obsession, and betrayal was continuous, even after the final verdict.

Avni walked through the quiet streets of Pune, the early morning haze softening the cityscape. Her mind wandered to Vihaan Palkar, the cricketing prodigy whose disappearance had sparked the investigation. For years, his legacy had been shrouded in mystery, speculation, and silence. Now, the truth had emerged, vindicating his courage and exposing the sinister forces that had tried to silence him.

She remembered the abandoned cricket bat, its worn wood engraved with clues that only someone determined and perceptive could decipher. That bat had been more than a relic; it was Vihaan's final attempt to leave a trail, a beacon guiding her investigation through shadows of corruption and fear.

As she passed by cricket grounds and empty stadiums, Avni reflected on the lives intertwined with Vihaan's story, coaches who had been silenced, journalists who had hesitated, and ordinary citizens who had become unwilling witnesses. The city's collective consciousness had shifted, realizing that passion for the sport could no longer be separated from accountability, ethics, and integrity.

Rakesh joined her, carrying a folder of final documentation. "The board has announced reforms," he said quietly. "Financial transparency, match oversight, and whistleblower protections. It won't undo the past, but it's a start."

Avni nodded, feeling a mixture of satisfaction and melancholy. Justice had been served, yet the personal cost, the sleepless nights, constant danger, and emotional strain, had been enormous. She thought of Vihaan and smiled faintly. "He finally gets the recognition he deserves," she said softly. "Not just for the cricket, but for standing up when it mattered most."

The sun broke through the haze, illuminating Pune in a soft, golden light. Avni felt the city breathe anew, a place scarred by corruption but capable of redemption. Her journey had ended for now, but the lessons, the truths uncovered, and the legacy of courage would resonate far beyond the headlines.

Avni approached the Pune Cricket Museum, its historic façade bathed in the afternoon sunlight. Inside, the atmosphere was hushed, respectful, a sanctuary for stories of triumph, struggle, and legacy. Today, the focus was singular: Vihaan Palkar's abandoned bat, finally preserved as a symbol of courage and truth.

The curator led her to a glass display case. The bat rested on a velvet cushion, its worn wood illuminated by a soft spotlight. Tiny engraved markings, once overlooked or dismissed as mere scratches, now told a story of defiance and persistence. Each initial, date, and symbol had guided Avni through weeks of investigation, serving as a quiet witness to Vihaan's struggle against corruption.

Visitors paused reverently, reading plaques that explained the bat's significance. It was more than a cricket artifact, it was a testament to integrity, resilience, and the enduring power of standing up for what is right. For the younger generation of cricketers, it symbolized that talent alone was insufficient; ethics and courage were equally vital.

Avni lingered, recalling moments of danger and doubt during the investigation, the threats, the near misses, and the constant weight of responsibility. She traced her fingers along the glass as if reaching out to Vihaan himself. "This is for you," she whispered. "Your story isn't forgotten. Your truth has reshaped the game."

The curator smiled softly. “Many have followed this story, but few understand its full impact. Today, Pune remembers not just a cricketer, but the values he stood for.”

Avni stepped back, allowing other visitors their moments of reflection. She felt a sense of closure and fulfillment. The investigation was complete, justice served, and the legacy of Vihaan Palkar immortalized. The bat, silent yet powerful, would inspire generations, a reminder that courage and truth could outlast fear and corruption.

Leaving the museum, Avni felt a rare calm settle over her. The intensity of weeks spent chasing leads, analyzing evidence, and navigating threats had left her drained, but the sense of purpose and achievement lingered. She walked through Pune’s bustling streets, observing life resuming its rhythm, yet changed in subtle ways.

The investigation had transformed her, not just professionally, but personally. Avni had confronted fear, uncertainty, and moral dilemmas, pushing herself beyond limits she had never imagined. Each challenge had strengthened her resolve, sharpened her instincts, and clarified her commitment to truth.

Her phone buzzed with messages: colleagues congratulating her, former mentors praising her diligence, and even some of the witnesses thanking her for protecting them. Yet, amidst the recognition, Avni remained grounded. She knew the work was bigger than accolades; it was about integrity, accountability, and the courage to act when the stakes were highest.

She reflected on the countless nights spent tracing Vihaan's clues, the abandoned bat that had ignited the investigation, and the layers of corruption she had exposed. Every piece of evidence, every careful verification, and every strategic move had been essential in dismantling Singh's network. The experience had taught her patience, vigilance, and the power of persistence.

As she paused by a quiet park, Avni allowed herself a deep breath. The city had changed, cricket had changed, and she had changed. Yet, she realized that this was not the end, it was a milestone. The fight against corruption, greed, and betrayal was ongoing, and the responsibility to uphold truth was constant.

Avni straightened, resolved and invigorated. The city of Pune, the sport she loved, and the legacy of Vihaan Palkar now stood intertwined with her own story, a testament to courage, resilience, and the enduring pursuit of justice.

Back in her office, Avni sorted through the remaining files and notes from the case. Though the investigation had concluded, the patterns of corruption she had uncovered lingered in her mind. Every ledger, every coerced witness, every shady transfer had been a piece of a larger, more pervasive network. She knew vigilance had to continue, this victory was important, but it was only one battle in a long war.

Rakesh entered with a tentative smile. "The team has been talking," he said. "We're proud of what we accomplished. But everyone feels the need to keep pushing forward. There's more work out there, other cases, other systems that need scrutiny."

Avni nodded thoughtfully. "Yes," she said. "This case showed me that corruption rarely exists in isolation. It's systemic, layered, and often hidden behind power and prestige. The victory here is symbolic, but our work must continue. The lessons we've learned, the strategies we've developed, they can be applied elsewhere."

Sunil chimed in, reviewing digital evidence protocols. "Our methods for securing data, verifying sources, and anticipating sabotage have been tested to the limit. We now have a blueprint for tackling complex networks efficiently and safely."

Kavita added, "And the media response proves that timing, coordination, and public awareness are critical. We've learned how to balance transparency with security, ensuring both impact and protection."

Avni leaned back in her chair, considering the future. Her journey through Vihaan Palkar's story, the dismantling of Singh's network, and the protection of witnesses had been transformative. She felt a renewed sense of purpose, this was not just about reporting the news or exposing wrongdoing; it was about creating lasting change.

She picked up her pen, opening a fresh notebook. Notes for a new investigation, new leads, and emerging stories awaited. Pune had been restored in one sense, but the fight for justice never truly ended. Avni smiled faintly, energized by the knowledge that her next challenge was already waiting.

Avni sat alone in her office as evening settled over Pune. The city outside glowed softly with streetlights, but inside, the quiet gave her space to reflect on the personal cost of the investigation. Weeks of sleepless nights, constant tension, and the ever-present threat of retaliation had taken their toll. Her body felt exhausted, and her mind carried the weight of near misses, dangers, and moral dilemmas.

Yet, alongside the exhaustion was an undeniable sense of growth. Avni realized she had become more resilient, decisive, and confident in her abilities. She had learned to anticipate moves, manage risks, and navigate complex human behaviors, skills that would serve her in any future endeavor. Each challenge, each threat, and each victory had shaped her, forging a sense of purpose stronger than any fear.

Her thoughts drifted to Vihaan Palkar. He had stood alone, confronting forces far larger than himself, and in doing so, had created a path for truth to emerge. Avni felt a deep respect for his courage, understanding that his silent perseverance had been instrumental in shaping the outcome. His legacy would live on, not only in the cricketing world but in the lessons of integrity and bravery he left behind.

Rakesh and Sunil had been invaluable, their technical expertise and unwavering commitment providing a foundation for success. Jamkar's vigilance had ensured safety at every turn, and Kavita's media coordination had amplified their efforts to a public level. Avni realized that courage alone could not have achieved this; collaboration, trust, and meticulous planning had been equally vital.

As she closed her eyes for a brief moment, Avni felt a profound sense of closure. The battle had been difficult, and the journey transformative. But she knew one thing: this was not the end. The lessons she had learned, the courage she had witnessed, and the truths she had uncovered would guide her in every future pursuit of justice.

Weeks later, Avni found herself in a sunlit classroom at Pune's premier journalism institute. Young aspiring reporters sat eagerly, notebooks open, pens poised. Their eyes reflected curiosity and ambition, but also the uncertainty that came with entering a field often fraught with ethical dilemmas and hidden dangers.

Avni began her lecture, recounting her journey through the Vihaan Palkar investigation and the dismantling of Vikram Singh's syndicate. She emphasized the importance of evidence, verification, and meticulous planning. "Courage is essential," she said, "but without preparation, strategy, and collaboration, it's wasted."

The students listened intently as she described the challenges faced, intimidation, legal roadblocks, and the emotional strain of pursuing justice against powerful adversaries. She explained how each member of her team had played a vital role: technical experts, legal advisors, media coordinators, and security professionals. The lesson was clear: investigative journalism was never a solitary pursuit.

One student raised a hand. "How did you stay motivated when the threats felt overwhelming?"

Avni paused, choosing her words carefully. "I thought about the people affected, the truth that needed to be revealed, and the legacy of courage left behind by individuals like Vihaan Palkar. That purpose, combined with trust in your team and meticulous planning, will carry you through even the darkest moments."

After the session, several students approached her privately, inspired and eager to learn. Avni smiled, realizing that the lessons from this case would ripple far beyond Pune, shaping a new generation of journalists committed to truth and integrity.

As she left the classroom, she glanced at the city skyline. Pune had changed, its institutions strengthened, and its citizens more aware. And Avni knew her journey was just beginning, mentorship, advocacy, and vigilance were the next steps in ensuring that courage, truth, and justice would continue to thrive.

Avni returned to the old Pune stadium, now quiet and largely empty, its floodlights switched off, casting long shadows across the stands. The familiar scent of dust, leather, and worn wood filled the air, bringing back vivid memories of her investigation, the late-night chases, secret meetings, and the adrenaline-fueled moments of discovery.

She walked along the pitch, pausing at the spot where Vihaan Palkar's abandoned bat had been found. That bat had been the catalyst, the silent guide through layers of corruption, betrayal, and danger. Avni knelt and ran her fingers along the ground, imagining the determination and courage it had taken for Vihaan to leave behind clues that could eventually expose the syndicate.

The stadium, once a backdrop to secrecy and power plays, now seemed almost sacred. Each creaking plank, each worn seat, had witnessed history in its own way, the triumphs of players, the shadows of corruption, and ultimately, the unveiling of truth. Avni felt a sense of closure, knowing that the place that had held so many secrets was now part of a story of justice and integrity.

She reflected on her own journey, the exhaustion, the fear, the victories, and the lessons learned. The investigation had tested her limits, but it had also strengthened her resolve and clarified her purpose. Every challenge had been a step toward ensuring that courage and truth prevailed over intimidation and deceit.

As she stood, sunlight filtered through the stadium arches, casting a warm glow on the pitch. Avni allowed herself a moment of gratitude, for Vihaan, her team, the witnesses, and even the city that had borne witness to the unfolding drama. The battle was over, but the lessons would remain.

With one last glance at the stadium, Avni turned and walked away, carrying not just the memories of a hard-fought investigation but the inspiration to continue pursuing truth, justice, and integrity wherever the path might lead.

Back in her office, Avni spread out the remaining files and notes from the Vihaan Palkar case. The investigation had ended, yet its echoes lingered, patterns of corruption, greed, and manipulation revealed systemic weaknesses that could reemerge elsewhere. She knew her role as a journalist was far from over.

Rakesh leaned against the doorframe, holding a fresh stack of investigative leads. "There's chatter about another potential scandal," he said cautiously. "Different sector, but the patterns are eerily similar. If we act fast, we could prevent a lot of damage before it escalates."

Avni nodded, already thinking strategically. "We learned so much from Singh's network, how they operate, cover tracks, and intimidate. This knowledge gives us a significant advantage. But we have to be meticulous. No shortcuts, no assumptions. Every step must be verified, every source cross-checked, and every backup secured."

Sunil chimed in from his workstation. "Digital evidence protocols are ready. We can monitor leads, secure communications, and ensure redundancy for every document. The technology now gives us a safer and more efficient way to investigate."

Kavita added, “And the media impact plan can be applied again. Strategic timing, verification, and public engagement, it works if coordinated properly.”

Avni took a deep breath, feeling the familiar spark of determination. The Vihaan Palkar investigation had been transformative, teaching her resilience, strategy, and the power of teamwork. Now, it was time to apply those lessons to new challenges, ensuring that truth and justice continued to prevail.

She opened a fresh notebook, jotting down preliminary notes for the next investigation. Each lead, contact, and observation was cataloged carefully. Pune had been restored in one sense, but the work of vigilance and accountability was ongoing. Avni smiled faintly, invigorated by the possibilities ahead, the fight for justice was far from over.

Avni sat at her desk as dusk settled over Pune, the city glowing softly through her office window. The journey through the Vihaan Palkar investigation had left an indelible mark on her life. She thought of the risks she had taken, the sleepless nights, and the constant tension, yet she also reflected on the courage, collaboration, and meticulous planning that had turned danger into triumph.

She remembered the abandoned cricket bat, the clues it held, and the silent guidance it provided. Vihaan’s courage had sparked a chain of events that reshaped the city’s cricketing and political landscape. His legacy was no longer shrouded in mystery, it had become a symbol of integrity, resilience, and the power of truth.

Looking at the stack of completed reports, Avni understood that her role was more than a career, it was a responsibility. Each investigation, each story, was a chance to expose injustice, protect the vulnerable, and inspire others to act with courage. The lessons from this case, the necessity of preparation, the strength of collaboration, and the importance of vigilance, would guide her forever.

She smiled faintly, imagining the students she had mentored, the journalists she had inspired, and the citizens now aware of the importance of transparency and accountability. Pune, the city she had fought for, had been transformed, and the story would resonate for years to come.

Avni leaned back, allowing herself a moment of quiet pride. The battle had been grueling, the stakes monumental, but justice had prevailed. The city, the sport, and the people who had trusted her would remember this effort. And as she turned her attention to the next investigation, she knew one truth above all: courage and truth were timeless, and the pursuit of justice would always endure.

The city lights twinkled outside, a reminder that life moved forward, but the impact of her work, and Vihaan Palkar's legacy, would continue to illuminate the path for those brave enough to follow.

CHAPTER : 15

NEW BEGINNINGS

The morning sun poured through Avni's office window, casting long shadows over stacks of reports and notebooks. Though the Vihaan Palkar investigation had concluded, her mind was already racing ahead. Patterns of corruption rarely existed in isolation, and whispers of another brewing scandal had reached her ears. The city's pulse was alive with opportunity, and Avni could sense that the next story would demand every ounce of skill, strategy, and courage she had honed.

Rakesh sat across from her, coffee in hand, reviewing preliminary documents. "The intel we've received is credible," he said quietly. "It involves multiple layers, financial irregularities, potential collusion in municipal projects, and some key figures with political influence. The complexity rivals the Palkar case."

Avni leaned forward, her eyes narrowing as she processed the information. "Good. Then we approach it the same way. Evidence first, verification second, and any exposure, timed and precise. This isn't just about uncovering wrongdoing; it's about ensuring it can't be brushed aside or covered up."

Sunil, already scanning digital records, added, “We have the protocols and redundancy systems ready. Every document, transaction, and communication will be secure. If this network tries to manipulate or intimidate, we’ll be prepared.”

Kavita chimed in, “And media coordination will be crucial. Early transparency, factual reporting, and strategic release of verified information will shape public perception while maintaining safety for all involved.”

Avni exhaled slowly, feeling a familiar surge of focus and determination. The stakes were high, but so was the opportunity to make a tangible difference. Lessons from the Palkar case, the importance of meticulous planning, teamwork, and courage, would guide them.

She opened a fresh notebook, pen poised. This was the beginning of a new chapter, a fresh battle against corruption, deceit, and greed. Pune had taught her that vigilance never rested, and neither would she.

Avni gathered her core team in the small conference room, walls lined with whiteboards, corkboards, and digital screens displaying streams of data. The room hummed with quiet intensity. Each team member knew the stakes: this investigation required precision, foresight, and airtight execution.

“First,” Avni began, pointing to a map of Pune on the wall, “we identify the key nodes, people, organizations, and accounts that form the backbone of this operation.

Nothing is too small to examine. Patterns in one sector can reveal networks in another."

Rakesh nodded, adding, "We've already cross-referenced public records, financial statements, and municipal contracts. Certain inconsistencies suggest deliberate obfuscation. It's subtle, but when traced methodically, it becomes visible."

Sunil projected a series of encrypted spreadsheets onto the screen. "Every digital trail will be secured, duplicated, and monitored for any tampering. We're implementing multi-layered verification and redundancy, lessons we learned from Singh's network."

Kavita chimed in, "Media strategy will run concurrently with the investigation. Verified findings will be released incrementally to maintain credibility, create public awareness, and prevent disinformation campaigns. Timing is as critical as accuracy."

Avni paced slowly, letting the weight of responsibility sink in. "This is about more than exposing wrongdoing. It's about systemic change. If we succeed, we not only uncover a network of corruption but also create mechanisms to prevent its recurrence. That requires discipline, discretion, and foresight."

The team exchanged determined glances, fully aware of the dangers ahead. They would face intimidation, misdirection, and perhaps threats to their safety, but the plan was set: evidence first, strategy second, exposure last.

Avni finally sat, opening her notebook to a clean page. She began jotting down the first steps, contacts to approach, data points to secure, and preliminary analysis priorities. Pune had once again become the battlefield of truth, and this time, they would be ready from the very beginning.

The team moved swiftly into the field, their movements precise and calculated. Pune's streets were alive with activity, markets bustling, vehicles honking, and the hum of daily life masking the clandestine work unfolding behind closed doors. Every footstep, every conversation, and every observation mattered.

Avni and Rakesh started by visiting municipal offices, quietly requesting records and cross-referencing public contracts with financial data. They noticed subtle discrepancies, suspicious approvals, unexplained budget allocations, and intermediaries who had no official authority but appeared repeatedly in transactions.

Sunil worked on-site with encrypted laptops, capturing data from public terminals, scanning for hidden links, and establishing a secure, offline repository. Each file was meticulously verified and backed up to multiple secure servers, ensuring redundancy in case of interference.

Kavita coordinated media monitoring from a mobile command setup. She tracked social media chatter, local news reports, and public statements from officials, identifying patterns that could indicate leaks or attempts at misinformation. Early detection of these signals would be critical to maintaining control of the narrative.

Avni paused at a quiet corner near a municipal office, reviewing notes and aligning the team's observations. "This network operates in layers," she said. "On the surface, it appears legitimate, but the connections beneath reveal intent and coordination. Every detail we capture is a thread that, when pulled, will unravel the whole structure."

Hours passed, and the first significant lead emerged: a series of shell companies linked to municipal contracts, all funneling funds through the same set of intermediaries. The pattern mirrored techniques used in previous corruption cases, confirming that this network was sophisticated yet vulnerable to systematic analysis.

For Avni, the thrill of discovery was immediate and precise. They were no longer reacting; they were dictating the pace of investigation. Pune had once again become a city of secrets, and Avni's team was prepared to uncover them, one lead at a time.

The following day, Avni and her team intensified their investigation, tracing the shell companies and intermediaries uncovered in the previous sweep. Each link led to another, a complex web of financial transfers, business fronts, and opaque agreements. Pune's cityscape, bustling and ordinary, masked the hidden networks of influence operating just beneath the surface.

Rakesh mapped the connections on a digital board. Lines and nodes formed a sprawling diagram, showing relationships between intermediaries, minor officials, and corporate entities. “These people aren’t acting alone,” he said. “Someone at the top orchestrates this, ensuring each layer remains insulated from scrutiny.”

Avni nodded, examining the evidence closely. “Exactly. And the top layer is our primary target. The intermediaries are predictable, they make mistakes, leave traces. If we can map these accurately, we can identify the real power brokers behind the network.”

Sunil cross-checked bank statements and digital communications. Subtle patterns emerged, repetitive timestamps, mirrored transfers, and recurring names in unrelated transactions. Each anomaly pointed toward influential figures who, publicly, maintained impeccable reputations. Behind closed doors, they manipulated projects, skimmed funds, and orchestrated approvals for personal gain.

Kavita continued monitoring media and public sentiment. “There’s chatter online about delayed municipal projects, procurement irregularities, and unexplained budget shifts. It’s subtle, but it confirms our suspicions, there’s a broader narrative forming, and public awareness is slowly growing.”

Avni stood, connecting pieces on the board with a sharp pencil. “We need to approach this strategically. Identify the key intermediaries, understand their behavior patterns, and trace every connection upward. Once we reach the top, we will have undeniable evidence of orchestration, not just opportunistic corruption."

The team worked late into the evening, layering evidence and refining strategies. Each revelation fueled determination. Pune's hidden networks were formidable, but the team had the expertise, discipline, and vision to uncover the truth. With every lead, Avni felt the investigation gaining momentum, an intricate puzzle slowly revealing the full picture of corruption and deception.

By mid-afternoon, Avni's team had identified a key figure whose influence permeated the network: a senior municipal official with longstanding ties to prominent business entities. Publicly, he was respected, a figurehead of development projects and civic initiatives, but the evidence suggested he was orchestrating approvals, channeling funds, and shielding intermediaries from scrutiny.

Rakesh traced a series of complex financial maneuvers. "These transfers are layered," he explained. "Funds are routed through multiple shell companies, some registered abroad, before returning as payments to local contractors. It's sophisticated, but the patterns are consistent. And the official we identified is at the center of it."

Sunil cross-verified communications, uncovering encrypted emails and coded messages between the official and intermediaries. The messages contained subtle instructions, timing cues, and financial directives, leaving a digital footprint that linked the figure directly to the operations.

Avni leaned over the board, analyzing the connections. “This is our breakthrough,” she said. “Not just because of his position, but because exposing him publicly will have a domino effect. Once we prove his orchestration, the intermediaries and lower-level operatives will be compelled to cooperate or face accountability.”

Kavita monitored online platforms, observing early hints of public interest and curiosity. “There’s rising chatter,” she noted. “People are noticing discrepancies in municipal projects, funding gaps, and unexplained delays. If we release verified findings strategically, it will strengthen public support and protect our investigation from being undermined.”

Avni paused, reflecting on the parallels with the Vihaan Palkar case. Courage, meticulous planning, and precise execution had dismantled Singh’s network. Now, the principles were being applied again, adapted to a more complex civic and political landscape.

With renewed determination, she assigned tasks: Rakesh to track financial layers further, Sunil to secure digital evidence, Kavita to monitor public narratives, and herself to connect each piece strategically. The first major breakthrough had been achieved, but the path ahead would require precision, patience, and vigilance, the stakes had never been higher.

As evening descended over Pune, Avni's team began discreet surveillance on the municipal official. Their approach was methodical, tracking meetings, monitoring communications, and observing patterns without revealing their presence. Each detail could provide crucial evidence to confirm his orchestration of the network.

Rakesh coordinated the financial monitoring remotely, flagging transactions that matched previously identified patterns. "These small, frequent transfers are likely bribes or kickbacks," he noted. "They're structured to avoid immediate detection, but the repetition and timing are consistent with the official's known activities."

Sunil set up secure digital surveillance, monitoring emails, encrypted messaging platforms, and online transactions. Any attempt to hide or delete data would now be recorded, timestamped, and stored in multiple secure locations. Redundancy and verification were key to ensuring the evidence would withstand scrutiny.

Kavita monitored media coverage, social chatter, and potential leaks. "Rumors about sudden project delays and questionable approvals are spreading organically," she reported. "If we time our disclosures carefully, we can control the narrative while maintaining our credibility."

Avni stood at the edge of the operation, observing the official leave a government building. She noted his patterns, routes taken, meetings attended, and associates encountered. Each movement added clarity to the network, revealing how influence flowed through intermediaries and into projects across the city.

Hours of surveillance yielded critical insights: the official's reliance on intermediaries, his predictable timing, and subtle communication signals. Every observation was meticulously logged, cross-checked, and backed up, forming a comprehensive record.

By nightfall, Avni reviewed the team's findings. "We're building an airtight case," she said. "Each detail, each transaction, each meeting strengthens our evidence. Precision now will give us leverage later. The network may be sophisticated, but diligence and strategy will uncover the truth."

Late that night, as the city lights flickered across Pune, Avni pored over the surveillance logs and financial patterns. A subtle, previously overlooked link emerged, a shell company tied to the municipal official had financial interactions with a high-profile business tycoon, known for his influence across civic and industrial sectors.

Rakesh highlighted the connections on the digital board. "Look here," he said. "These offshore transfers route through multiple intermediaries before entering the tycoon's accounts. It's a complex laundering operation, but the pattern is consistent with the official's manipulations."

Sunil cross-referenced communications, uncovering coded messages exchanged between the official and the tycoon's aides. Timing, phrasing, and instructions confirmed coordination, revealing a previously hidden layer of the network. The tycoon wasn't just benefiting financially, he was an active participant, ensuring the municipal projects were manipulated to serve his own business interests.

Kavita leaned forward, her eyes sharp. "This changes the stakes," she said. "We're no longer dealing with a single corrupt official. This involves someone with immense influence, media sway, and political connections. Exposure must be precise, verifiable, and strategically timed to prevent obstruction or retaliation."

Avni nodded, absorbing the gravity of the revelation. "Exactly. But this also gives us leverage. The tycoon's actions are traceable, and the intermediaries leave trails. If we proceed carefully, we can dismantle both layers of the network, holding the orchestrators accountable while protecting witnesses and evidence."

The team spent hours mapping every transaction, every meeting, and every digital footprint. Connections previously invisible became clear, forming a network of influence, power, and illicit coordination. Each piece of evidence reinforced the others, creating a robust foundation for the next phase of the investigation.

Avni paused, looking at the illuminated map of Pune. The city seemed ordinary, yet beneath its surface, a web of corruption was exposed. For her and her team, this discovery marked a turning point, the investigation had escalated, but with strategy, courage, and meticulous planning, they were ready to confront the tycoon and the network he controlled.

The following morning, Avni called a strategy meeting. The team gathered around the large digital map and evidence board, each member focused on the task ahead. The discovery of the tycoon's involvement meant the stakes had escalated significantly; meticulous planning and airtight evidence were essential.

"We need hard proof," Avni began, her voice calm but resolute. "Financial trails are strong, but we require real-world confirmation, contracts, memos, recordings, anything that directly links him to the manipulations. Digital evidence alone can be challenged, but multiple forms of corroboration will make the case unassailable."

Rakesh reviewed the financial network. "I can track suspicious transactions further, connecting the tycoon to intermediaries, municipal accounts, and offshore entities. Each layer adds weight, but timing and synchronization are critical to avoid detection."

Sunil added, "We'll need surveillance in key locations, business offices, meetings, and transport routes. Any interaction with intermediaries, contractors, or officials could yield visual or digital proof. Our methods must be covert; even the slightest misstep could compromise everything."

Kavita leaned forward. "I'll monitor media and public signals. We need to anticipate leaks, narrative manipulation, or attempts at preemptive discrediting.

Timing of disclosures will be crucial once we have irrefutable evidence."

Avni studied the map carefully, marking locations, intermediaries, and potential vulnerabilities in the tycoon's operations. "Coordination is key," she said. "Every move we make must be synchronized, digital, physical, and informational. The tycoon's influence is extensive, but so is our preparation. We stay methodical, we stay patient, and we stay ahead."

As the team nodded in agreement, Avni felt a familiar surge of determination. Pune's hidden networks were complex, but diligence, strategy, and courage had brought them this far. The next phase would be the most challenging yet, but Avni knew that with meticulous planning, the network's exposure, and justice was within reach.

By mid-afternoon, Avni's team began the first phase of field operations. Pune's streets and business districts, bustling with activity, concealed the meticulous surveillance they had planned. Every movement was calculated, every observation intentional, and every detail recorded.

Rakesh coordinated from a mobile command center, tracking financial interactions and monitoring communications between the tycoon and intermediaries. Each anomaly was highlighted and cross-referenced with prior intelligence, ensuring no opportunity went unnoticed.

Sunil deployed discreet cameras and monitoring equipment near key offices and meeting locations. Digital logs, timestamps, and encrypted backups were maintained meticulously. Each piece of real-time evidence added to the growing body of data linking the tycoon to the network.

Kavita tracked social and mainstream media for signals, rumors, leaks, and public chatter, that could indicate attempts at misinformation or preemptive damage control. Timing was critical; any premature exposure could alert the tycoon and compromise the investigation.

Avni herself moved through the field, observing interactions, noting patterns in behavior, and recording critical details in her notebook. She recognized subtle cues: the timing of meetings, the body language of intermediaries, and repeated behaviors that suggested coordination and control.

By evening, the team had collected enough preliminary evidence to establish the tycoon's active involvement. A combination of digital trails, physical surveillance, and indirect confirmations from intermediaries painted a clear picture. The network was vast and sophisticated, but their systematic approach had begun to unravel it.

Avni gathered the team to review the day's findings. "We're building a compelling case," she said. "Each observation, each recorded interaction, strengthens our position. Patience and precision have brought us this far. Tomorrow, we escalate, targeted surveillance and direct evidence gathering. Every step must be measured, deliberate, and coordinated."

The team nodded in unison, their focus sharpened. Pune's hidden network was starting to crack, and with determination and strategy, they were poised to expose the tycoon's orchestrations fully.

The following morning, Avni and her team executed a carefully planned operation to secure direct evidence of the tycoon's involvement. Every move had been coordinated in advance, timing, positioning, and contingency plans were synchronized to minimize risk and maximize results.

Sunil monitored encrypted communications and live feeds, alerting the team to any suspicious activity. "He's meeting with an intermediary now," Sunil whispered. "Looks like discussions about project allocations and financial transfers."

Rakesh focused on tracking documents and transactional evidence, ready to intercept contracts, invoices, and emails that could corroborate digital trails. Each file captured would add irrefutable weight to the case, leaving no room for plausible deniability.

Avni positioned herself discreetly near the meeting location, noting the interactions, the tycoon's gestures, coded language, and subtle exchanges with his aides. Every movement was cataloged meticulously, each observation reinforcing the network's orchestration.

After hours of patient observation, the breakthrough arrived. The intermediary handed a folder to the tycoon, and covert surveillance captured the transaction, including signatures and internal memos referencing diverted funds. This was the first indisputable proof directly linking the tycoon to illegal operations.

Kavita, monitoring public chatter, confirmed that no premature leaks had occurred. "We're still under the radar," she noted. "The information is secure, and the narrative is controlled."

Avni allowed herself a small, satisfied smile. "This is it," she said. "Direct evidence, corroborated and verifiable. From here, we can connect every intermediary, every transaction, and every project back to him. The network is starting to unravel."

The team exhaled collectively, the tension of days of surveillance giving way to cautious optimism. Pune's hidden structures of corruption were being exposed, one deliberate, strategic step at a time, and Avni knew they were poised for the next critical phase, solidifying the case and preparing for the ultimate confrontation with the tycoon and his network.

CHAPTER : 16

CONFRONTATION AND RESOLUTION

The city of Pune had changed. The streets hummed with the usual rhythm of life, yet beneath the ordinary bustle, a reckoning was underway. Avni sat in her office, reviewing the meticulously compiled evidence against the tycoon and his network. Months of surveillance, financial tracing, and strategic planning had brought them to this moment. Every intermediary traced, every document verified, every conversation recorded now formed an unassailable case.

Rakesh entered with a sense of controlled urgency. “Avni, we’ve cross-checked every detail. From the tycoon’s offshore accounts to the municipal approvals, everything aligns. There’s no gap, no ambiguity. We’re ready.”

Sunil added, “Digital and physical evidence are secured, encrypted, and backed up. Even if someone tries to manipulate the system, there’s no way to compromise the integrity of what we’ve gathered.”

Kavita leaned forward, eyes serious. “Media strategy is in place. Verified leaks, timed release, and public transparency. Once we go live, the narrative will shift in our favor, leaving no room for misinformation or counter-attacks.”

Avni inhaled deeply, feeling the weight of responsibility, tempered with determination. “This is more than exposing a network, it’s about accountability at every level. The intermediaries, the politicians, the tycoon, they all must face consequences. And we must ensure the system learns from this, so corruption cannot flourish unchecked again.”

The city skyline glimmered outside the window, reflecting the possibilities that lay ahead. Pune, with all its vibrancy, complexity, and hidden layers, had become a battleground of truth. And now, the culmination of months of meticulous work, courage, and resilience was within reach.

Avni looked at her team, seeing focus, loyalty, and shared determination mirrored in their eyes. “This is the moment we’ve prepared for. Let’s bring it all together, justice, transparency, and accountability. The city deserves no less, and history will remember the courage it took to uncover the truth.”

The following day, Pune’s administration building became the center of a calculated storm. Avni and her team coordinated with law enforcement, ensuring that every arrest, search, and seizure was executed with precision. The tycoon, once untouchable, and the municipal official who had facilitated the network were cornered, their influence unable to shield them from the mounting evidence.

Rakesh oversaw the transfer of financial records, contracts, and communication logs to authorities. “Everything has been verified and cross-checked,” he said. “No discrepancies, no gaps. It’s airtight.”

Sunil monitored digital channels, confirming that encrypted backups were secure and that no evidence could be tampered with during the operation. “Even if they attempt interference, it won’t matter. The records are preserved in multiple locations,” he noted.

Kavita coordinated the media narrative. Verified reports were prepared for simultaneous release, ensuring transparency and public awareness. By controlling the narrative, they prevented misinformation and maintained public confidence in the process.

Avni stood in the operations room, her eyes fixed on live feeds. The tycoon and his associates were escorted out of the building, their previously untouchable aura shattered. Their faces, once symbols of power, now reflected shock, disbelief, and inevitability.

Police carried out the arrests methodically, ensuring compliance with legal protocols. The intermediaries were questioned, and additional evidence linking political figures emerged, confirming suspicions and tightening the network’s exposure.

As cameras recorded the unfolding events and news outlets prepared bulletins, Avni allowed herself a moment of quiet satisfaction. Months of preparation, strategic planning, and unwavering perseverance had culminated in this moment, justice finally reaching those who had long operated above accountability.

The city of Pune watched as the balance of power shifted. Corruption had been exposed, and transparency had triumphed. For Avni, it was the culmination of her journey, proof that courage, strategy, and integrity could overcome even the most formidable networks of deceit.

Night had fallen over Pune, but the city felt different, lighter, almost as if a weight had been lifted. Avni sat at her desk, reviewing the final reports and press coverage. The tycoon and his accomplices had been arrested, their schemes laid bare, and the municipal network had been dismantled. Justice, painstakingly earned, had prevailed.

She reflected on the journey, the long nights, tense surveillance, and strategic maneuvers. Each risk had been calculated, every lead verified, and every decision weighed against the potential consequences. The investigation had tested her resolve, intelligence, and moral compass, yet it had also revealed the strength of teamwork, perseverance, and courage.

Avni thought of her team: Rakesh's analytical brilliance, Sunil's technological precision, and Kavita's media acumen had all been indispensable. Each had contributed not only skill but loyalty and unwavering commitment.

The success was theirs collectively, a testament to collaboration under pressure.

Her mind wandered briefly to the Vihaan Palkar investigation months earlier. Patterns, lessons, and strategies had been refined, applied, and expanded. The principles of meticulous planning, ethical vigilance, and strategic exposure had proven effective once more. Courage combined with preparation could indeed bring down networks that seemed untouchable.

Looking out over Pune's skyline, Avni felt a sense of closure yet anticipation. The city had changed, institutions strengthened, and citizens more aware of accountability. Yet she knew vigilance was eternal; corruption and deceit could emerge again. Her role as a journalist, mentor, and guardian of truth was ongoing.

A small smile formed on her face. The fight for justice was not just a battle but a legacy, one that she and her team had fortified. The city would remember this moment, but more importantly, it would inspire vigilance, courage, and integrity in those who dared to follow.

Avni turned off the lights, her resolve renewed. The story had ended, but the mission endured. Pune, the city she had fought for, was safer, wiser, and ready for the challenges ahead. And she would be there, ready to uncover the truth wherever it hid.

www.ingramcontent.com/pod-product-compliance
Ingram Content Group UK Ltd.
Pitfield, Milton Keynes, MK11 3LW, UK
UKHW040038200726
13845UKWH00054B/493

9 789334 439878